Bernie

Also by David Brelsford and published by Ginninderra Press
Crossroads

David Brelsford

Bernie

All royalties from the sale of this book will be donated to
the Motor Neurone Disease Association of Tasmania.

See page 150 for information about motor neurone disease.

Bernie
ISBN 978 1 76041 601 0
Copyright © text David Brelsford 2018
Cover photo: Berner Sennenhund sitzt in Dünen, by wuschelpfoten

First published 2018 by
GINNINDERRA PRESS
PO Box 3461 Port Adelaide 5015
www.ginninderrapress.com.au

Contents

Bernie

'What does your father do now he's retired?'

'He runs.'

'What?'

Sylvia smiled. 'Dad's one of these characters who's still running marathons at sixty-six.'

'Oh.' Maxine raised her eyes heavenwards in the universal show of disapproval.

'How do you think he'll react about us?'

Sylvia breathed out heavily and crinkled her brow. 'I don't know,' she said. 'He's always been very conformist, and since Mum died I think he's got worse. I'm a bit worried about it.'

'Well, if he doesn't like it, we'll leave.'

'We've come all this way to see my father. I'm not leaving within two minutes. And what about Bernie?'

'Yeah, Bernie could be a problem. We're going to need our negotiating skills, my love.'

Bernie was asleep in the back of the car, unaware that his life was about to change.

They drove up to Kevin Harper's place, in a quiet street backing on to bushland, and with a nervous sigh they climbed out of the car.

He was sitting on the veranda.

'He looks smaller than I imagined,' said Maxine.

He stood up as they met, gave his daughter a hug and shook hands with Maxine. 'Green tea?' he asked.

'What?'

'Would you like some green tea?'

'Er, have you got any ordinary tea?'

'Oh. Oh yes, I think I've got some somewhere,' as he rummaged through his shelves.

The girls exchanged glances and Sylvia pulled the corners of her mouth down.

'I hear you're a fitness – er – enthusiast,' said Maxine as they sat.

'I've been known to run a few marathons, yes.'

'Do you win any?'

He snorted quietly. 'Not at my age, but I occasionally get a place in my age group.'

Maxine couldn't help herself. 'Why do you do it?'

He had his answer ready for that. 'If I didn't, I'd be down the boozer every day getting drunk. Which do you prefer?'

And Maxine dropped her eyes.

And all three of them thought their breathing was a bit too loud.

'Dad,' said Sylvia finally, 'Maxine and I are going on a holiday together, six weeks in Europe.'

'Are you now.'

'We – um – we wondered if you could take care of Bernie for us while we're away?'

'Bernie? I've never met him.'

'Well, now's your chance. He's in the car.'

They walked out to where Bernie was still sleeping in the back seat.

'He's big, isn't he?' said Kevin Harper. 'How old is he?'

'Just two.'

At the sound of their voices, Bernie awoke and looked up.

'Say hello,' said Sylvia, and opened the door.

Bernie jumped out and stood with his tail rigid and nose directed at Mr Harper's groin. His top lip trembled and his eyes did not blink.

Kevin Harper had the sense not to move.

'Offer him the palm of your hand to smell,' said Sylvia. 'He's okay. He's never bitten anybody yet.'

'There's always a first time,' said her father. 'But if he bites me, I'll shoot him.'

'He won't bite you. He's just weighing you up.'

And Maxine thought *I hope he gets a better opinion of you than I have.*

'What sort is he?'

'Bernese mountain dog.'

'And that's why you call him Bernie?'

'Yes.'

'I thought your mother and I had brought you up to be a bit more original than that.'

You bloody wanker, thought Maxine.

They walked back up to the house with Bernie's nose immediately behind the back of Kevin Harper's thighs.

'A dog understands tone of voice,' said Sylvia. 'Of course they'll learn individual words in time, but they recognise tone of voice and body language instinctively.'

So you've got no fucking chance, thought Maxine.

They walked up the steps to the veranda and into the house, Bernie following.

Kevin Harper looked round in surprise. 'Is he allowed inside houses?' he asked.

'He's allowed inside my house,' said his daughter.

'Our house,' corrected Maxine.

'What?'

'He's house-trained,' said Sylvia quickly.

'What do you mean, "our house"?'

'Yeah,' said Sylvia, breathing in deeply. 'Maxine and I are buying a house together.'

Mr Harper stood looking at them, waiting for more information.

Now or never, thought his daughter. 'Maxine and I are…partners.'

'Business partners?' he asked, although he knew the answer to that.

'No, Dad.'

Oh let him have it with both barrels, thought Maxine. 'No,' she said. 'Sylvia and I are sexual partners, Mr Harper.'

'Lesbians?'

'That's the word, yes. We prefer the word gay, however, which stands for "good as you".'

There was a pause, a very pregnant pause, during which Bernie growled quietly. 'I see,' he said at last.

Another pause.

'And you're going away together.'

'Yes.'

'And you want me to look after your dog?'

'His name is Bernie,' said Maxine.

'I know that!' he snapped.

'Dad,' pleaded Sylvia, 'we can't afford to put him in a kennel for six weeks. We'll pay you for the food. He's no trouble really once you get to know him.'

'And what about when I go out training?'

'He'd love to run with you, especially along those bush trails.'

Kevin Harper let out a big sigh and his shoulders relaxed slightly. 'Well, that's what parents are for, I suppose.'

'Mum would have loved it,' said Sylvia.

'Hm,' he said, with a slight nod.

Jump in while the iron's hot, thought Maxine. 'Let's drink to it,' she said. 'I don't suppose you've got any alcohol?'

He looked at her out of the corner of his eye. 'No,' he said quietly. 'I don't drink.'

Might as well throw the handle after the hatchet, she thought. 'Red wine is good for the heart,' she said.

He turned his back on her and contemplated Bernie the dog. 'Is he used to sleeping inside?'

'Yes. He usually sleeps in the kitchen. We don't allow him in the bedroom.'

He was tempted to make a sarcastic remark about males in their bedroom but thought it best not to. 'I've got some old blankets I can make up for him,' he said.

'Thanks, Dad,' said Sylvia and hugged him.

Maxine remained seated. 'We've brought some tins of dog food for him. But don't go running with him immediately after he's eaten or he may be sick.'

'I realise that!' he said. 'I have learnt a few things in my sixty-six years.'

And plenty still to learn, she thought; but kept quiet.

And while they were talking, Bernie sat with his tail straight, staring hard at the man who was to be his carer.

After they said their goodbyes, Kevin Harper stood and watched the car disappear into the distance. *Hmmph!* he thought. *They can afford to go gallivanting around Europe for six weeks but they can't afford to put it in a kennels. Foist it onto the old man, eh!*

He stomped back into the house, logged on to his computer and brought up Bernese mountain dogs. 'Bernese,' he read, 'are a big dog, larger than a German Shepherd but smaller than a Great Dane. They are outdoor dogs at heart. They need activity and exercise but do not have a great deal of endurance, preferring to run no more than about six kilometres each time. They do not usually self-exercise. They tend to bond with one owner.'

'This isn't looking good,' he said to the dog. 'I'm an endurance man who runs a damn sight more than six k per day. And I love to self-exercise. And you've no doubt bonded with Sylvia already, although hopefully not with that other silly woman.' He looked at the dog, who was listening intently. 'But at least we're both outdoor types, so I guess that's a start.'

He got up and opened the back door. 'I'll leave that open for you through the night. I'm not having you shitting all over the house. You're supposed to be house-trained. And tomorrow we'll go for a run and see what you're made of.'

In the morning before his alarm went off, he felt a cold touch on his cheek. He woke to see Bernie's nose next to his face, two big friendly brown eyes looking at him, and a wagging tail that said, *Come on, let's go!*

'Well, you're keen and no mistake,' he said to the dog as he dressed.

The morning was bright and cold with just a hint of frost.

'Should be just right for you,' he said. 'You're supposed to be a mountain dog. And me, I'll warm up soon enough.'

The back gate out of his block led into the bush, where the trails wound for over two kilometres before coming out onto a lonely gravel road. Bernie had kept close to Kevin as though he feared getting lost, and when they reached the road Kevin paused.

'If we turn round now, it'll be less than five k overall,' he said. 'Let's go a bit further.'

And Bernie, looking up at him, ran alongside without any effort.

'We'll turn at that house up there.'

But as they approached the solitary house, they heard a sound and suddenly there was a dog barking furiously at them from behind the fence.

'Shep! Shep! Stop it!'

Kevin stopped and stood with his hands on his hips, catching his breath, and a woman came out of the house to control her dog.

He had to laugh. 'You call it Shep?'

'It's a her.'

'And you call her Shep.' It was a statement now.

'Yes.'

'Well, calling a German Shepherd Shep is worse than calling a Bernese mountain dog Bernie.'

'I didn't give her the name. She was my son's.'

'Did he give her to you?'

'Yes, basically. He's joined the army. So I've inherited her. So don't blame me for calling her Shep.'

He lifted his chin in understanding.

'Anyway,' she continued. 'You can't talk, naming your Bernese mountain dog Bernie.'

'He's not mine. I'm looking after him while my daughter's away.'

'And she called him Bernie?'

'Yes.'

She chuckled. 'This younger generation,' she laughed. 'No originality.' But she said it affectionately. And for a brief second, her face was in danger of crumpling before she overcame it.

And while they talked, the two dogs were nose to nose through the fence, sniffing. Then the tails started to wag.

'I've seen you before,' said the lady. 'You run past here quite often.'

'Yes, I do.'

'Do you run marathons?'

'Yes.'

'Well, I won't be so foolish as to ask if you win, or why you do it, or even how long a marathon is.'

'Well, that's good to hear. You won't believe how many people ask me those sorts of questions.'

She laughed. 'Well, Toby – that's my son – was a very good gymnast and he used to run to get fit. Now he's in the army.'

And there was that hint of sadness in her voice.

He looked at the dogs. 'I don't think they'll fight if we let your dog out for a moment,' he said.

'Call her Shep.'

'Oh yeah, sure. Sorry.'

'Janice,' she said.

'What?'

'That's my name. Janice.'

He extended his hand. 'Kevin.'

The dogs' tails were waving happily now as they sniffed each other all over.

'I must go,' said Kevin Harper. 'Otherwise I'll start to stiffen up.'

'If ever you need a drink on your runs, just call in. You know now that Shep won't hurt you.'

'Thanks. Cheers.'

And as they ran away, Kevin said to Bernie, 'That was nice, wasn't it?'

And Janice said to Shep, 'Fancy a German Shepherd getting friendly with a Bernese mountain dog. What next, eh!'

When they got home, Kevin gave Bernie a drink and a biscuit. 'You're not so bad,' he said. 'You don't bark, you don't dig or jump and you're friendly with people and other dogs. Sylvia's trained you well.'

And Bernie, looking intently at him, wagged his tail furiously, and then promptly flopped over and went to sleep.

Kevin laughed. 'You're a comical bugger too, just quietly,' he chuckled.

He went to bed a little earlier than usual that night and set his alarm clock fifteen minutes earlier. When it went off, he swung his legs out of bed just in time before Bernie came trotting in. 'I beat you that time,' he grinned, ruffling the dog's ears.

He knew of course where he would run. But halfway along the bush tracks he suddenly realised that Bernie was not running beside him. *What's happened to him?* he thought as he backtracked. But there was Bernie, head down and snuffling enthusiastically at a hole in the ground.

'Come on, mate,' he said. 'We're supposed to be running.' And as they went along he said, 'I'll take you for a casual walk this afternoon so's you can explore the area properly.'

As they approached Janice's, he called out and Shep came running to meet her new friend.

Janice came out, flour over her hands. 'Hello, Kevin.'

'Hi, Janice,' he said. 'I want to run a bit further but I don't think Bernie will stay the distance. Any chance of leaving him here for half an hour and I'll pick him up on my way back?'

'Sure. And Shep will love it. I'll have a drink ready for you when you come back.'

A refreshing orange juice was waiting for him when he returned after running another seven k. He gulped it down gratefully. He looked at Janice. *Not a bad sort*, he thought.

'Maybe I can buy you a drink in a more civilised manner,' he said. 'Could I take you to lunch?'

And as she smiled, the two dogs were romping in the backyard, tumbling and racing like mad things.

The town where they lived was not big but it boasted a cosy little restaurant with a quiet atmosphere, and as they went in a Mozart serenade was playing.

'Do you like classical music?' she asked once they had ordered.

'Not particularly,' he said. 'I don't know much about it.'

'My husband used to play the clarinet. Not in an orchestra or anything, just for his own amusement.'

'Your husband?'

'He died two years ago.'

'I'm sorry.'

'What about you? You said you had a daughter.'

'Yes. My wife died six years ago. My daughter lives with her partner' – he mentioned a city two hundred kilometres away – 'but they've gone to Europe for six weeks.' He omitted to mention that his daughter's partner was another woman.

'So what do you do apart from running?'

He grinned. 'Eating and sleeping. No, I keep the place tidy – I enjoy gardening – but long-distance running does take up a lot of time.'

She nodded in understanding.

'What about you?' he asked.

'Well, since Gary – that was my husband – died, I concentrated on making sure Toby would be okay. But now he's joined the army, I'm at a bit of a loose end.'

'Is he happy in the army?'

'He seems to be. But I wish he hadn't gone. I miss him.'

'You've got Shep to keep you company.'

She smiled in agreement. 'She's really taken to Bernie,' she said. 'You should see them together.'

About a week later, Kevin woke to find that Bernie was not around. Where had he got to? Then he noticed that the back gate was open and cursed his carelessness in leaving it unlocked. But at least he knew where Bernie would be. He put on his running gear and headed out through the bush tracks and on to the lonely road to Janice's house.

It was quiet and he knocked on the door.

Janice came with a sombre face. 'Come in.'

'What's the matter?'

'Bernie came, late last night, I think. He's been with Shep all night. She's just come on heat, that's why he made it here fast. But…'

'But what? Where is he?'

'Kevin, I'm so sorry. Bernie got hit by a car early this morning. He's, well, he's dead. He's in the backyard.'

'Oh hell!' Kevin flung his head back. 'Oh hell! And I was getting to like him.'

'Let me make you a good cup of tea. Or would you like something stronger?'

'I don't usually drink but perhaps a little brandy in the tea might be good.'

He sat at the table and held his head in his hands while she busied herself. 'Hell,' he said again. 'What am I going to tell Sylvia?'

'Come here,' she said. She put her arms around him and held him tight. 'I'm sorry. I'm sorry.'

'You're not to blame,' he said.

'But I feel responsible.'

'No. Don't feel guilty. It was my fault for leaving the gate unlocked.'

'I think I'll have a brandy with my tea too.'

They buried Bernie in the backyard. 'He would have liked to rest near Shep,' said Kevin.

'Stay for lunch.'

'Thank you.'

It was a warm afternoon and they sat on Janice's back deck and observed Shep, lying contentedly on the lawn.

'You need to keep her enclosed now so that no other dogs can get to her.'

'Yes. She's had her share of loving for now.' She turned and looked at him with slightly moist eyes. 'But some of us haven't yet…'

It was late in the evening when Kevin Harper returned home and flopped on his bed.

'What a day. A friend lost and a lover gained. What am I going to tell Sylvia?'

He thought of sending her an email but decided not to spoil her holiday. *I'll tell her when she gets back*, he thought. *And anyway, email is a cowardly way to do it.*

Instead, an email came to him.

Hi, Dad, having a great time here. We've decided to stay for another four weeks because if we do we may be able to negotiate a business deal in Zurich. Hope you can look after Bernie for us a little longer. Bet he's loving running with you!

He couldn't resist a sigh of relief. *It lets me off the hook for a little longer.*

For the next few weeks, Kevin felt as though he was living on borrowed time. His visits to Janice were – to say the least – very pleasant. She was about ten years younger than him and two lonely souls found comfort, pleasure and occasional laughter in each other's company. In addition to that, it soon became apparent that Shep was pregnant.

'I'll give you one of the puppies,' said Janice.

'I wonder what they'll look like.'

'I figure they're due in four days' time.'

And Kevin Harper felt his stomach sink just a little. That was the date that his daughter was finally returning from overseas. *A grown man like me shouldn't be frightened of his daughter*, he told himself. And answered, *I'm not frightened. But I'm still not looking forward to it. Bernie was a nice dog.*

The phone rang late in the evening. 'Hi, Dad, we're home! How's Bernie?'

He still couldn't bring himself to tell her outright. 'Can I come down and see you?' he asked.

'Sure, Dad.'

'I'll start early in the morning and be with you by lunchtime.'

Click.

Alone in his car, he approached her town with trepidation. *Stop worrying*, he told himself repeatedly. *He was only a pet dog after all. She'll get over it*!

Sylvia greeted him with a hug and a kiss while Maxine merely nodded cordially and then disappeared into another room.

'Bad news, my dear,' he said. 'There's no easy way to tell you. Bernie was killed not long after you left. I'm sorry. I liked him.'

She moved slowly and her arms dropped by her side. 'Oh. Ah. Oh dear.'

'I'm so sorry,' he said. 'He was hit by a car. It was my fault, I'd left the back gate unlocked.'

The tears were in her eyes but she looked up at him. 'Dad, don't beat yourself up about it. We'll get another dog, eventually. But we've got a lot of things to catch up with. I was going to ask you if you could keep him for another couple of weeks anyway until we get back on an even keel.'

They sat down over a coffee. Maxine was nowhere to be seen.

'The meeting in Zurich means that I'll have a lot more work for a few weeks, which is good.' She paused. 'It'll help me take my mind off it.'

He was anxious to change the subject. 'How's Maxine?'

'Oh, fine. I think she's gone to bed. She enjoyed the trip, same as me.'

He was relieved to go and still felt as though he had let his daughter down. Well, at least he'd told her, he'd got that ordeal over. Tomorrow he would go to Janice's and see if Shep had whelped yet.

And there they were, just four blind squirming bundles of fur, with their mother jealously guarding them.

'How did you go with your daughter?' asked Janice.

He sucked in his breath. 'Cool,' he said. 'Definitely cool. She said all the comforting platitudes but I think she's really disappointed.'

Despite the novelty of the puppies, he was glad to get away. He felt as though he wanted to be alone for a while. He went for a good long run which left him tired but feeling more content. *The local marathon coming up soon*, he told himself. *Time to get some solid running in.*

And he retreated into his training. Rain, wind or cold, he was out there; paying his occasional visits to Janice; getting plenty of early nights and just superficially keeping in touch with his daughter. He got into the habit of running past Janice's house and calling out as he went past, then stopping for a quick drink on his way back.

But one morning, there was no one there. He thought little of it and finished his run.

But in the afternoon a knock came on his door. And there stood Janice, with a little bundle of fur in her hands.

'Can I come in?' she said.

When they were seated, she spoke. It sounded as though she had rehearsed it. 'Toby's injured himself. It happens a lot in the army, more than people realise. He's being invalided out. I'm going up to where he lives to look after him. He hasn't got a partner and he'll find it difficult to get one now.'

'What happened?' he asked.

'Something blew up in his face. He's lost the sight of one eye and most of his hearing. And the use of one arm.' And suddenly her shoulders collapsed and her face collapsed and she could hold herself in no longer. She wept and wept while Kevin held her tight.

'I'm sorry,' she said, sniffling. 'I'm sorry.'

'No!' he said. 'No. You need to cry. Don't hold it in.'

And she took comfort in his lean, hard body as he held her, while on the carpet the little bundle of fur squirmed and yapped.

'I promised you a puppy to replace Bernie,' she said eventually. 'Here he is.'

'A male! What a handsome little pup! Thank you so much. Has he got a name?'

'No. I figured it was up to you to give him that.' She paused. 'He'll be something to remember me by.'

He sat down and they held hands across the table. 'Life can be so hard,' she said. 'For a long time, I was happy with Gary and Toby. Then Gary died. Now Toby's like this.' She looked at him through her tears. 'I found comfort with you. Perhaps even love. I'm so grateful to you, Kevin.'

'We'll keep in touch,' he said. 'We'll email. And I'm sure we can meet up occasionally.'

She smiled and nodded. 'That will be nice. I'll look forward to that.'

She had her son to fill her life now. And Kevin, well, he had his running as always. And he knew what he was going to do with the puppy.

It was a long drive down to where his daughter lived and it was late afternoon when he got there. The two girls were relaxing after work when he arrived and presented them with Bernie's replacement.

'Oh, Dad! Thank you so much! I know you liked Bernie. This is so nice of you. We'll love him!'

'He's a cross between a Bernese mountain dog and a German Shepherd. Bernie was the father. He'll grow up to be a good strong dog.'

'What's his name?'

'I'll leave that to you. But can I ask you just one thing?'

'Yes?'

'Don't call him Toby.'

On his drive back home, he felt curiously free. He had lost Janice, true, but it had not been his fault. And now he had recompensed his daughter for the loss of Bernie. Even with his sadness over Janice, he felt at peace.

His training went well; he felt he was able now to give it his full concentration. And when the race came, he felt fit and confident. He started strongly and ran well through the bulk of the race, but with only five k to go his energy levels plummeted and all he wanted to do was stop. He forced himself to keep running. He just wanted to finish, that's all, he wasn't worried about his time any more. People at the side of the road applauded this elderly man still running marathons at his age. But they were applauding his age, not his performance. Coming in toward the back of the field, struggling just to keep going, he was overtaken by lots of other runners – teenagers running their first big race, a couple of men he knew he could usually beat – and then to his chagrin a walker with that comical waddle. With about a hundred metres to go, a man passed him running with a dog.

Labrador, he thought automatically.

He crossed the line and staggered to the side. *That was a bad run*, he thought.

As he stood with his hands on his knees, the Labrador came up and sniffed him, and then walked away.

'Tough race, eh,' said a voice. It was the owner of the dog.

He just had the energy to nod. 'You've got the dog to pull you along,' he said, managing a grin.

'Couldn't do it without Rex,' said the man. 'Y'see, I'm legally blind. Oh, I can see a bit but Rex always guides me in the right direction.'

'Good on him,' said Kevin Harper. 'And good on you too. You're an inspiration.'

And while they chatted, Rex the dog came and sniffed him again and then wagged his tail.

The next day, Kevin Harper felt totally depleted. It was not unnatural for him to feel that way after a marathon. He knew he would recover in a few days. He made it a point to have a sleep every day after lunch to let his body recover from the ordeal.

He had just woken up after his siesta when there was a knock on the door. Muttering darkly to himself, he answered it, and there stood Maxine.

'What brings you here?' he asked in genuine surprise.

'I've come to say thank you. May I come in?'

When they were seated in the living room, Maxine said, 'Sylvia is still madly busy with her new work arrangements. She wants me to tell you – and I'm telling you myself – how very grateful we are to you for giving us Fletch.'

'Fletch?

'That's what we've decided to call the puppy. He's absolutely beautiful. You know, Sylvia cried herself to sleep that day you told us Bernie was dead. She didn't let you see it, but she took it really hard. But Fletch has changed all that. She absolutely adores him. We both do.'

'And you've come all the way here just to say that?'

'Well, yes. But also to say I'm sorry we got off on the wrong foot, Mister Harper.'

'Call me Kevin.'

'I've come especially to say thank you and to hope that we can become friends. Sylvia and I really do love each other, you know.'

'Yes, I can see that,' he said, 'Now. I've experienced the pleasure and pain of love myself since you first brought Bernie.'

'He was a great dog, wasn't he?'

'He sure was. I owe a lot to him.'

'Well, Fletch is growing up in the same mould. We'll bring him to see you one day.'

'That will be good. And Maxine?'

'Yes?'

'I'm glad we're friends now.'

'Me too. You're not such a bad old stick after all,' she laughed.

'Let's drink to it. I do keep the occasional beer in the fridge now.'

As they sat with their drinks, he said, 'Did I tell you that I met a semi-blind man running with his dog in the marathon? It made me realise how lucky I am.'

She smiled and touched his arm in genuine friendship.

When she was gone, he said, *Well, that was great.* And suddenly he realised he was talking to himself. No Bernie, no Janice, no puppy. The silence seemed to echo.

But he knew what to do about it.

When he awoke the next morning, it was pouring rain. He thought briefly about staying in bed, but forced himself to get up. He had things to do.

Instead of going through his back gate into the bush trails, he headed out the front, onto the street and down the hill towards town. By the time he got to the shopping centre, he was wet through. He ran grinning past the townsfolk scurrying between the shops under their umbrellas. He ran through to the other side of town and kept going. About two kilometres along, he swung into Sandstone Road and then a little later he turned into his destination.

Soaked to the bone, he wiped his face and stepped into the office. The girl on the counter looked up at him. Behind her on the wall, the sign said RSPCA.

'Morning, miss,' he said. 'Do you have any dogs available for adoption?'

Burning Bridges

They've done it again! Just as we were about to catch them, they ran across this bridge and now we can't cross it because of fire.

We danced in rage, rattling our spears, but they stood and laughed at us.

'You're primitive,' they shouted. 'You're savages. You'll never catch us.' And they disappeared into the bush on the other side of the river.

We sat down, tired after our unsuccessful pursuit.

'This is the third time they've done that,' I said. 'We must find an answer.'

We discussed the problem and many ideas were put forward. Most of them wouldn't work. But I thought mine would. We argued about it but as the leader I insisted that we try my plan.

So late that night, three of us swam the river and went into the forest. We saw the lights of our opponents' camp and skirted around it. We kept on going. By early morning, we had reached our destination. We rested for a couple of hours and then started preparing.

It wasn't long before we heard the sounds of pursuit. The second part of our plan was working. The rest of our party had crossed the river and were now chasing our adversaries towards me and my two helpers.

We waited. The sounds grew closer.

'Ready,' I said to my men, and the bridge over the chasm behind us was suddenly unpassable because of fire.

When our opponents reached us, they stopped and stared.

'Now we have you,' I gloated.

They looked around wildly. Our party was closing in from behind and fanning out to each side to cut off their escape.

'You're surrounded,' I called. 'Admit defeat! And you must pay the price. Surrender!'

We were already looking forward to the spoils of victory.

Their leader came up to me and symbolically laid down his spear. 'Okay, you crafty devil,' he said. 'You got us this time. You win. Now let's get these fire notices down and get back. I guess our team owes your team a beer.'

Cliffs of Fall

I can assure you unequivocally and without the slightest shadow of a doubt that I am not, repeat not (and I use that word confidently), in any way shape or form or looked at from any angle in the spectrum of the compass, or looked at from any direction upwards sideways or downwards, or in any way shape or form (and I have repeated that because I want to emphasise it), but I am not and never have been and probably never will be mad.

Some people think I am but I am not. Not really. I let them think that way because it serves my purpose.

Ha!

I let them think that way because it serves my purpose, and I know I said that already but I want you to get it into your brain, to imprint itself into your grey matter so that you don't forget it, so that you remember it all the time while you hear my story.

Because I'm not mad. I just let people think I am.

Ha!

It's warm here and I get three meals a day and they let me watch television or read a book if I'm good, which I am most of the time, and I'm enthusiastic to tell them that it's warmer here than in Antarctica and they laugh and say anywhere is warmer than Antarctica and I let it go at that, ignorant people, because they've never been to Antarctica like I have so they don't know for sure, do they, it's only what they've read in books or seen on the TV but I know for sure because I've been there so I know.

Oh, Jefferson was a ratbag of the first degree but he wasn't fooling me, not for one minute, don't you worry about that. I saw through him in the first couple of days so that's why I started going out alone, which you should never do in Antarctica because you never know what will happen. You could fall down a crevice or get caught in a blizzard and you should always put in the logbook what you're going to do but I didn't do that either because I didn't want him, Jefferson the ratbag, to know what I was up to.

It was the gulls. The gulls were mine. Yes. They were my babies and Jefferson didn't know and I had no intention of telling him, well, not straight away. I knew I would have to tell him eventually and I did but not till later and it was all his fault really so he got what was coming to him anyway, the ratbag.

Ha!

And Sonya too, stupid girl. Not a brain in her head but plenty of female hormones coursing through her body and that's what undid her in more ways than one, if you get my drift, because Jefferson the ratbag certainly undid her in more ways than one within the first couple of days, or should I say nights, and she didn't seem to object. In fact, she positively enjoyed it from what I can gather and I gathered a fair bit, don't you worry about that.

It wouldn't have worried me too much to tell the truth. What people get up to with their trousers down is no concern of mine but Jefferson was my boss and I would have to tell him eventually about the gulls and I didn't like the idea of toadying up to a lecher. The ratbag had never even glanced at me – well, not in that way – but as soon as he saw Sonya, you could just about hear the testosterone bubbling up inside him like the water on the stove when we made our cups of coffee before going out on the surveying trips and when he told me that I needn't come on the trips but could do my own research while he went on the trips with Sonya, well, it wasn't hard to work out what they'd be up to once my back was turned, was it?

I reckon they made up a lot of those statistics from their trips because they wouldn't have had the time to do it properly if they were shagging all the time. There, I've said it. Shagging.

Ha!

But bugger their shagging, if you'll excuse the French, because it gave me time with the gulls on the cliff, which is what I wanted and I knew I was doing valuable work, not like old Romeo and Juliet ,which is what I got to calling them, not to their faces of course, I'm not stupid, but they never asked me what I was doing while they were out there shagging on the ice, well, not on the ice literally, use your brains, they'd put up a tent and then into it!

Ha!

But the gulls were mine, yes all mine, and nobody else knew about them, not Romeo and Juliet or the other scientists Terry and Tim. They weren't interested at all, they were only interested in each other outside of their work, faggots, and that left me with the gulls my babies and the reason they were my babies is because nobody else knew about them except me, yes me, the only person on the whole surface of the planet who knew that the gulls on that cliff were of a variety never known before to the human brain and I wanted to preserve them because I knew what would happen as soon as word got out that this little group of scientists in this little outcrop of Antarctica had discovered a new breed of gull.

Well, it wasn't the little group, was it, it was just me. The others were too busy billing and cooing and shagging and doing whatever faggots do – I don't want to think about that, I just wanted the gulls to be safe from human intervention because people would come with their cameras and equipment and start taking eggs and killing them just to see what made them different and we would get smarmy documentaries made about them, how much we could all learn from them and all that bullshit when all they wanted was to be left alone to live and breed and die like they had done for thousands of years before humans ever came to this godforsaken place which is not fit for human habitation anyway. We should leave it to the gulls and the penguins and go back to where we came from where we could meet decent people not faggots or lechers who can't get their minds above their waists.

Anyway it had to happen sooner or later that I had to tell Mister Lover Boy about the gulls, he was my boss wasn't he, and he wanted to know what I had been doing with my time, so I told him and I reckon he told his fancy lady straight away and they wanted to come and have a look at the gulls, my gulls, my babies.

Well, I'm not stupid, don't you worry about that, so I didn't take them to the cliff where the gulls, my gulls, were nesting, I took them to another cliff which was far more dangerous and when they started to climb down I said goodbye to them and then I helped them down, if you get my drift, and I thought that was appropriate because the real Romeo and Juliet had died too, if I remember my Shakespeare correctly. And I do, of course.

Ha!

So when I told ol' Tweedledum and Tweedledee, which is what I called Terry and Tim, they came rushing as if they could do anything for them, but they were well and truly dead and had been as soon as they hit the bottom, don't you worry about that.

And that's when things started to work out perfectly because after the inquest and all that garbage when I didn't pull any punches about what I'd done and everybody thought I'd done it out of jealousy, the authorities decided to close down our little outpost, they reckoned it wasn't viable any more or some bullshit like that, and Terry and Tim got transferred to another research station and never knew about the gulls and I'm the only one who does and it's good that they put me in here, because no one will believe what I say anyway, so it's all worked out for the best.

I get three meals a day and I'm warm in here and I don't have to worry about anything. The gulls are safe, because nobody takes any notice of what I say, and that suits me fine.

I'm not an attractive woman and I never was. I got my science degree and went to Antarctica and I don't regret what I did. I have saved those rare gulls from all the nastiness of man's encroachment.

So I feign insanity because that's my little contribution to the welfare of the world.

And is it worth it? I like to think so.

Crumbling Barriers

It's not often that the village idiot is praised as the hero of the community. Aloysius Day was not really an idiot in the strict sense of the word. Al – which is what everyone called him – was just a bit slow but he wasn't stupid. As someone once said, 'He's got all his marbles. They just don't roll very smoothly.'

He did gardening jobs around the town and sometimes forgot to ask for payment. Some people, like Mrs Jones, would chase him through the main street insisting that he take the money she owed him. Others, like old man Withers, grinned slyly into his lukewarm soup and figured he'd diddled the simple fellow out of a few more precious dollars.

Truth was, dollars weren't precious to Al. He was pretty well off, just quietly. He didn't spend much; he got some sort of a pension – his gardening money was what they call the 'cash economy' – and he lived a very simple, uncomplicated life. When he wasn't mowing someone's lawn or sauntering through the shopping centre, everyone figured he was sitting at home playing silly computer games or watching daytime television. Little did they know what he was really up to when no one was watching (or caring).

Al may have been a bit slow but he wasn't stupid, and he had all the feelings and fantasies of a twenty-something young man. And that can be dangerous in someone who, with all due respects, has little or no chance of having a relationship with a girl in the normal way.

After the whole affair was over, it transpired that Al had been stalking young Elle for a long time, at least a year, ever since she was sixteen. This was delicate ground. A slightly retarded man, a young Aboriginal girl, and her extended family from the edge of town:

resentful, surly, and ready to take offence at any sideways glance cast their way. They kept to themselves and shunned the 'plurry whites' just as much as they were shunned.

It was wrong, of course. Both sides knew that. With some sensible work and tolerant cooperation, they could have worked together and been a much happier township. But no one was willing to take the first step. And the longer it went on, the harder it got, until everybody accepted that there was no hope. Just keep to ourselves, they all said. Nobody's fighting even if nobody's loving. We're getting along okay side by side.

But love, if that's what you want to call it, doesn't recognise skin colour or cultural differences. Al admired Elle from afar; you could hardly call it love since they never spoke to each other, and that was dangerous in itself, because it meant that Al conjured up beautiful conversations in his own mind and then persuaded himself that they had really happened.

And it must be said that Elle was a nice-looking young Aboriginal girl. But at seventeen years of age she was hardly old enough to become the serious partner of anybody, least of all a white man who was too doe-eyed and dreamy to be taken seriously.

Elle knew what Al thought of her. But she had seen first-hand the standing that the Aborigines had in the town and she had no doubts about the attitude that would be taken if trouble arose. She was an intelligent girl, quiet, modest and sober; she disagreed with those of her extended family who always blamed the whites for everything. She was sure she could rebuff any untoward advances Al might make; she felt a certain pity for him, that poor, slow, harmless man.

Not so Keppel Vaughan. Kep was a big man, bluff and hearty; the more malicious ones in town thought he was a bit of a loudmouth, but underneath it all they recognised an honest soul. He coached the local football team and although he drove them hard he made them play fair – and he let them know what idiots they'd been when they lost!

And Kep fancied Elle too. And while Al had been quietly stalking

Elle for a year but had done nothing further than that, Kep had only recently discovered her and taken to following her whenever he got the chance.

Kep would often walk around with a gun in case he saw a wild animal he could shoot. On this fateful Saturday, the sun shone hot and hard as it can only do in the Australian summer. Kep was out in the bush, striding along, head held high, chest puffed out, hoping to see something to shoot. He thought he would walk to the big rocks near Koala Creek and then take a short rest.

The two big rocks towered, double the height of a man even of Kep's size. There was a narrow fissure between them: too narrow for a person to fit in but an ideal haven for small creatures such as lizards, grasshoppers and snakes. The local Aborigines regarded it as a sacred site. Perhaps they saw the two rocks as some sort of yin and yang, a partnership of man and woman.

But such symbolic thoughts were far from Kep's mind as he approached the rocks. He was feeling the heat and looking forward to a sit down. But when he reached the clearing he suddenly stopped. There was the object of his fantasies.

Elle!

And with her was Aloysius. Innocent Al had finally plucked up the courage to speak to her, and Elle felt no danger from him. She figured if she was nice to him, that would be sufficient and he would eventually go away.

She stood with her back to the rocks and Al stood facing her. He wasn't too close. He was chatting pleasantly, telling her how hot it was (as if she didn't know) and warning her of the dangers of walking around barefoot (as if she didn't know!).

Suddenly! Suddenly! A sharp report, a puff of dust, and the two of them were on the ground screaming in pain.

Keppel rushed forward, his eyes were wide and his forehead creased. 'Are yous okay? Are yous okay?'

'My leg! My leg!' This was Elle.

'What?'

'You shot me in the leg!'

Meanwhile, Al was lying looking up at the sky with both hands over his left hip. His face was white.

'Are you okay, Al?' said Kep.

Al didn't reply. He lay gasping, his hands still over his hip.

'Let's have a look, Al.'

'What about my leg!' cried Elle.

Kep ignored her for the moment. At least she was conscious. But Al was worrying him. 'Al! Let me look at your hip!'

And slowly, Al turned his face towards Keppel and let him take his hands away. The bloody mess underneath made him shudder.

'You've been hit in the hip. Don't move!'

Elle got off the ground and hit him feebly on the back. 'What did you shoot us for? We weren't doing anything!'

'I wasn't shooting you. I was shooting at a snake near you. The bullet must've bounced off the rock.'

'Get me to hospital.'

'Yes! Yes!'

Keppel steadied himself. Fortunately he had his mobile phone with him and within a few minutes paramedics were carrying the two of them out to the nearby ambulance.

The head paramedic stopped for a brief moment and looked back at Kep. 'You're in deep shit, matey,' he said.

Now that the pandemonium was over, Kep sat on a stump and lit a cigarette. But within seconds he had thrown it down and was vomiting. His face was white and he trembled. 'I didn't shoot them!' he said to himself. 'I didn't shoot them!'

Two months later, he was saying the exact same words to the judge and jury. The courtroom was full; many locals had come along for the entertainment: this was the most exciting thing that had happened in town for years.

'I didn't shoot them,' said Keppel Vaughan. 'Not deliberately, I mean. I was shooting at a snake that was threatening them and the bullet bounced off the rock.'

Counsel for the prosecution looked over his glasses at Kep with an expression of disbelief.

'Look, mate,' said Kep – and the lawyer flinched at the familiarity – 'I'm a pretty good shot, and I was close to them. If I'd wanted to deliberately shoot 'em, I would've done a better job than that.'

'Perhaps you only ever intended to wound them,' said the lawyer. 'As a warning to keep away from each other.' He leaned forward. 'So that you could step in, Mister Vaughan!'

'No! I tell you I was shooting at a snake.'

'Hmmph,' came the reply. 'And in the process you took a slice out of the young woman's thigh and hit the man in the hip. She's going to have a scar, and he's going to be walking with a limp for the rest of his life. And you want to tell me it was an accident.'

'It *was* an accident!' Keppel was close to tears.

Some of the baser people in the courtroom smirked to see this self-styled macho man in such a state. But they weren't worried about their future. Kep could see an abyss opening before him and he didn't like it.

Counsel for the defence, Mr Robert Harley, stood up. 'Your honour,' he said, 'I would like to ask the court's permission to escort the jury to the scene of the alleged crime.'

'Is that necessary, Mr Harley?'

'Yes, your honour. I want to reconstruct what happened that day.'

'Very well.'

And as arrangements were made for the jury to visit the rocks, Kep turned to his lawyer. 'What's going on?'

'Don't worry about that now. I know what I'm doing.'

Within an hour, the jury, along with all the officials of the court, were assembled at the rocks. Again it was hot and men swatted flies.

'I won't keep you here too long,' said Harley. 'Now, would the three of you please stand where you were when the shot was fired.'

When this was done, he said, 'Look carefully and consider the facts.

Miss Elle suffered a flesh wound on the outside of her right thigh. Mr Day suffered a more serious wound in the left hip. But it is evident even from photographs, never mind the doctor's report, that the bullet entered Mr Day's hip from the front. Just how could Mr Vaughan have shot him from the front when Mr Day had his back to him? There is only one explanation, and that is that the bullet hit the ground, bounced up to the rock, ricocheted off the rock, grazed the girl's thigh, and then entered Mr Day's hip. There is no other way it could have happened.'

Harley pointed at the rock. 'If you look carefully,' he said, 'You can see the mark on the rock which the bullet made. It ties in exactly with what my client has been saying all along.'

It was time for the prosecuting lawyer to step forward. He looked at the rock, looked over to where Kep was still standing, did some simple calculations regarding distances and angles, and spoke. 'Let's get out of here,' he said. 'It's too hot.'

In the vehicle that took Keppel back to the courtroom, he sat with his head between his knees.

'It's going to be all right, Mr Vaughan,' said his lawyer.

'Yes,' said Kep. 'I'm just sorry for that poor bugger Al. He'll never walk properly again, and he was doing nothing wrong.'

'It won't be that bad. He'll have a limp but he'll still get around as well as ever.'

After that, it was just a formality that Kep was acquitted and released from custody.

He sat in Robert Harley's office ready to pay his fee. 'You lawyers certainly know how to charge,' he said. 'How much am I up for?'

'Nothing.'

'What?'

'That's all been taken care of.'

'It can't be!'

'Your fee has been paid by an anonymous person.'

'Who?'

'I'm not at liberty to disclose that. The person asked me not to tell you.' The lawyer shuffled his papers and seemed to come to a decision. 'I cannot tell you who paid your fee,' he said. 'It's all in the paperwork here but I can't show you. Now if you'll excuse me for a moment, Mr Vaughan, I have to visit the toilet.' And he walked out, leaving the papers in full view on his desk.

Now Keppel Vaughan may have been chastened by his ordeal but he was still alert enough to realise what the lawyer was really doing. And as he quickly looked at the paperwork he gasped to see who had paid his fee.

Aloysius Day!

'But he was supposed to be against me,' he thought.

Back at his home, he sat down and tried to figure out why his adversary had paid for his lawyer. 'I know what everybody thinks about Al,' he said to himself, 'But he's not stupid. And more importantly, he's not mean. He worked out what had really happened. But he knew they wouldn't take much notice of him. And they'd take even less notice of Elle. It needed someone with authority. He paid this Harley fellow to defend me and prove my innocence.'

He thought about Elle and realised how brave she had been. She held no grudge. Her thigh had healed and she knew that Kep had tried to save them from the snake. And he thought about Aloysius, that generous young man who had placed justice above personal revenge. And he knew that tomorrow was going to be a busy day.

Early in the morning, he called on Al and they had a long conversation together.

Later, he drove round to the town hospital, because there were a couple of bills he wanted to pay.

In the afternoon, he was back in the lawyer's office. 'I want to surrender my gun. Can you arrange that for me?'

'Certainly, Mr Vaughan. But are you sure?'

'Positive. I've no use for it any more.'

And towards evening, after showering and shaving, he drove to the Aboriginal sector of town where he knew Elle would be.

He was there for a long time and as he left he looked up at the eucalypt trees, smelt their sharp odour, and smiled as a wallaby hopped in front of him. 'My God, I love this country,' he said.

It is strange that even in a small town, some facts become general knowledge while others, just as equally available, never seem to take off. After a while, everyone knew that Al had paid for Kep's lawyer; but no one seemed any the wiser as to who had paid Al's and Elle's hospital bills.

All of that was some three years ago. Kep and Elle have a lovely daughter now, called Bonny, and it is increasingly apparent that she'll soon be having a brother or sister. They are a model family. And this family are proving to be a mediating force between the two cultures. No longer do they scowl at each other. In addition to the regular football team, Kep is coaching an all-Aboriginal team, and has even persuaded the art gallery to show some local native paintings.

He has his own landscape and gardening business now, and his best employee is the man called Aloysius Day. He's the real hero of the piece. Kep recognises that; he asked Al to be the godfather of Bonny, and Al has never been happier. Sure he walks with a limp, but he still gets around and he loves to play with baby Bonny.

Sometimes the four of them – Kep, Elle, Al and baby Bonny – go to the big rocks and have a picnic. And sometimes a few Aborigines join them. And over the last few months, some of the regular townsfolk have gone along too.

The barriers are starting to crumble!

Desolate Is a Beautiful Word

'But señoritas, the gringo trail does not go to the Altiplano,' said the guide.

'Good. Then we'll go.'

'But señoritas, it is cold up there. And barren. And poor. You would not like it.'

'We'll decide that. Here's the money we owe you. Now bugger off!'

The tattered Bolivian guide took the money and reluctantly lurched away. The two gringo women were mad, he thought. Why would they want to go up to the Altiplano? Far better to stay here in La Paz, with its nightclubs, its brothels and its relatively easy life. The gringos were arrogant too, he thought, like all gringos. But they paid well. What was it they said they were? Not Americans, but something like that. Australian, that was it. Whatever it was, he thought, they were mad to go up the Altiplano.

The two Australian girls organised horses and food and set off towards the Altiplano.

'Am I glad to be getting off the gringo trail!' said Helen. 'It was really beginning to bug me.'

'Yes,' said Sue. 'I think every white person that's ever been to Bolivia has visited all the same places and done all the same things. No wonder it's called the gringo trail.'

'Well, the Altiplano will be different,' replied Helen. 'Not many gringos come up here, by all accounts.'

'I'm not really surprised. It does look barren. It would have to be about the poorest area of the poorest country in South America.'

'What will we do when we get there, Sue?'

'Recover, for a start. Then I guess we'll just bum around as usual. We might even get a job.'

'Not much chance of that. Even the natives are flat out making a living without letting a couple of bludging gringos take their jobs.'

'We're both good cooks, though. You never know. And if we don't like it, we can always go back to La Paz,' said Sue. 'We're off the gringo trail for a while anyway. At least when we get back to university we can say we roughed it on the Bolivian High Plateau, even if it's only for a couple of nights.'

The Bolivian Altiplano – the High Plateau – is some fourteen thousand feet above sea level. The air is thin and cold, the soil is poor and rocky, and the natives scratch a miserable living on small subsistence farms, raising beans, potatoes and maize. The only 'good' time is during the harvest season, when for a few weeks at least there is the certainty of regular employment and sufficient food. Some of the farms hire up to twenty peasants for harvesting and, for the short period of the picking season, house them in cold and draughty dwellings and provide them with meals.

Thus it was that the two Australian girls stumbled across employment as cooks to some dozen or so pickers, on a typical Andean farm of the region.

The farm was typical, that is, in all but one respect. It was run by a woman. And what a woman!

'She's worse than the sports mistress back in uni,' quipped Helen.

They quickly coined a nickname for her. The Sour Señora. It was the aptest title they could have given her.

As soon as the first light of dawn appeared on the horizon the Sour Señora would be abroad, screaming at the girls to 'Hurry! Hurry! There are hungry workers waiting for a big breakfast! Hurry!'

The fact that the hungry workers were still snoring their heads off never seemed to occur to her.

'Hurry! Breakfast will be late! They have a hard day's work in front of them.'

They had a hard day's work in front of them all right, with the Sour Señora cajoling, haranguing and threatening them all day long as they laboured, bent-backed, under her merciless eye.

'But why does she lock everything away after every meal?' exclaimed Sue as they sat peeling small wormy potatoes. 'If she left stuff available so that we could prepare things in advance, we'd be a lot better off – and so would she.'

Helen nodded. 'She's got a phobia about losing things – or having them stolen.'

'She's nuts,' said Sue.

'She's a bitch,' said Helen.

'She's ugly,' said Sue.

'What she needs is a good man,' said Helen.

'No chance of that,' said Helen. 'Not with a character like hers.'

'How long are we staying in this job?'

'Couple or three weeks. We need the money.'

'I'm almost looking forward to uni,' said Helen.

'She's a bitch.'

'She's ugly.'

'She's nuts.'

Beans, potatoes and poor, mealy corn. An unending succession of meals. A couple of times, they scrounged some eggs, until the Sour Señora caught them.

'Do not steal my eggs!' she screamed. 'Do not give them to the workers! You are thieves! Gringo thieves!'

'Oh, go and stick your eggs, you silly old bitch,' said Sue in English.

'I forbid you to use my eggs again. You must not steal!' And with that she marched off, lipstick, mascara and fat, to supervise her slaves.

'Why is she so obsessed with people taking things from her?' said Sue.

'I wonder if anybody ever took her virginity,' smirked Helen.

'Speaking of that,' said Sue, 'there's a couple of pickers seem to be eyeing us up and down very closely.'

'I wouldn't mind,' said Helen. 'I'm feeling a bit deprived.'

'Helen! Not with a native!'

'Why not? They're still male.'

'Maybe it's time we were getting back on the gringo trail.'

Helen laughed. 'Yes, maybe. Still, it's been an experience, hasn't it? Let's see if we can steal another couple of eggs.'

Off they went to the fowl pen, where half a dozen starved, scrawny hens battled to keep their heads by producing the occasional egg. Down on their hands and knees, peering into the gloomy corner where they knew the eggs would be, they found two and backed out. As they did so, a sudden gust of wind blew dust and grit into their faces and made them duck their heads, oblivious for a few seconds of the world around them. A frightened, panicked hen battered itself against them as they wiped the dust from their eyes and nose.

'What wouldn't I give for a good hot bath,' groaned Helen.

'I wish I was lying on Bondi Beach right now,' said Sue.

'I always thought Manly Beach was better,' said a voice behind them. A male voice!

They spun.

'Who the hell are you!?'

'Paul Castle's the name. Late of Sydney. Manly Warringah to be exact,' he grinned.

'What are you doing here? How long have you been here? How did you get here? How are you earning a living? What…?'

'Hold it! Hold it!' he laughed. 'Come inside, I'll tell you.'

They made to go in the kitchen.

'No, not in there,' he said. 'This way.'

He led them through a door and into a room they had never seen before. By Altiplano standards, it was luxurious. Two armchairs, a double bed, red drapes and a threadbare red carpet.

'This is fantastic,' said Helen. 'How long have you been here?'

'About six weeks.'

'But how come we've never seen you before?'

'Ah. The madam – I believe you call her the Sour Señora – keeps me locked up.'

'What!?'

'Oh, it's voluntary on my part. I just remain out of the way. She likes it like that.'

'She likes everything locked up,' said Sue.

'But what are you doing here?' asked Helen.

'I'm, er, well, I suppose you would call me Madam's lover.'

There was a slight pause and then both girls started giggling. 'You're the Sour Señora's lover? Oh, what a laugh! No wonder she keeps you locked up. She's afraid you'll get stolen too.'

He was grinning himself.

'But why, Paul? Why?'

'Well…' he put his hands behind his head and leaned back. 'I guess it was just another easy way out.'

'What do you mean?'

'I said I come from Manly Warringah. Palm Beach to be exact. My father's a lawyer. I am an only child. I've had it easy all my life. Parties, dances, the beach, good food, everything provided. I've been to New Zealand, America, Europe, England, Mexico, Hawaii – and now South America.'

'But why the Altiplano?'

He shrugged. 'Same as you, I suppose. Just wanted to get off the gringo trail for a while. Only I couldn't get a job. Oh, I wasn't short of money – I never have been – but when I happened on to this farm, the Madam took a liking to me and told me she'd feed me if I became her lover. I thought it would be a laugh for a while. That was about six weeks ago.'

'And is it still a laugh?'

He smiled. 'It's starting to wear a bit thin,' he admitted.

Sue and Helen looked at each other, then back to Paul. All three of them had the same idea.

'Let's get the hell out.'

'Yes.'

'When?'

'Tonight. After the evening meal.'

'Can't,' said Paul. 'The Madam will be with me as soon as the meal's over.'

'Okay, tomorrow then, when they're all in the fields.'

'Right.'

'Hey, Paul,' said Helen as they prepared to go, 'take it easy with the Sour Señora tonight. After tomorrow you've got two of us to keep satisfied, you know.'

When they had gone, Paul Castle, the son of a Palm Beach lawyer, lay back on the couch. I must have been born under a lucky star, he thought. Two of them! This will be something to tell the guys when I get back. I'd better take a couple of raw eggs.

The Sour Señora (lipstick, mascara and fat) was her usual high-pitched, possessive self. 'Hurry, hurry!' she screamed at them when the meal was over. 'Hurry to wash the dishes. Then I lock up.'

'Yeah,' said Sue in English. 'And now we know why you're in a hurry, you old bitch.'

The Sour Señora bustled to and fro, sweated, swore and stumbled in a frantic rush to get everything locked up.

'It's a wonder she doesn't lock the toilet,' said Helen.

'You do not steal any more of my eggs!' was the Sour Señora's parting shot as she closed the door.

'We're stealing more than your eggs tomorrow, you old cow,' said Sue to the closed door. 'Poor Paul. Imagine having to make love to that!'

Helen giggled quietly. 'You know,' she snickered, 'I'm quite looking forward to tomorrow night.'

'So am I,' said Sue. 'And Paul will be too. It'll be a real orgy.'

*

The armchair sagged as the Sour Señora lowered herself into it. 'Ah, Paul, my dear, those two girls from your country are very rebellious. They do not like me and they insult me in their own language.'

Paul brought her a drink, then sat in the other armchair. He said nothing.

'They are very young,' said the Sour Señora.

Paul said nothing.

'And beautiful,' she said.

The wine was very pleasant and revived her spirit a little after her exhausting day. Paul refilled her glass.

'Thank you, my love,' she said.

He sat down again.

'The Australian girls are young and beautiful,' she repeated, but Paul only nodded vaguely and kept silent.

'But they do not know you are here,' she said.

He smiled for her. And for himself.

She inhaled to speak again but suddenly Paul said, 'Tell me, why do you have two chairs here? And why a double bed? Do you always employ a paid lover?'

I am very cruel, he thought.

But she showed no sign of resentment. Only wistfulness. 'Ah, it is a beautiful room, is it not? There is not another one like it on all the Altiplano.' Her eyes were above his head but they were looking into the past. 'My husband designed it and furnished it. He knew how to make me happy.'

'Your husband?' said Paul incredulously.

'Yes. He was a very good man. He designed this room. He knew I loved red. His name was Gonzalo. We were so happy.'

'What happened to him?' asked Paul quietly.

She gritted her teeth as if to brace herself against pain. 'They took him and accused him of growing drugs. And my son too.'

'Your son?'

'Yes. He was only fifteen. But they took him and his father.' She spat. 'We never grew drugs. But they didn't care. They just wanted someone to arrest. My husband and son were innocent. What do you call them? Scapegoats.'

The tears ran mascara down her greasy cheeks. She bent her head to try and hide her grief from her lover. Now I am old and fat, she thought, and I have to pay a gringo to make love to me. But it was not always so.

She raised her head again. 'We were so happy,' she said. 'And I was beautiful in those days. Everyone said we were the handsomest family on the Altiplano. Our son would have inherited the farm, and Gonzalo and I had this room. Now,' she sighed, 'now it is like a shrine to our happiness.'

'Then why do you desecrate it by having a gringo lover?'

Why do I have to be so cruel? he thought.

'Ah, Paul,' she said. 'My dear Paul, you do not understand. They took away my husband and my son and left me desolate.' She got up and moved over to the bed. 'But I am still a woman who gets lonely and who needs a man.' She touched the bed lovingly. 'Many times my Gonzalo and I made love on this bed. My son was born here. Everything important that has ever happened to me has happened here.' She looked tenderly at the bed again.

Paul put down his drink and got up. That's a cue if ever there was one, he thought as he moved towards her.

*

After breakfast, Paul and the girls caught a chicken, chopped its head off and stuffed it into a bag, stole some more eggs, then galloped away rapidly while the workers were in the far field. They rode hard for a long time until they got to the edge of the Altiplano. Then in a little town, they sold their horses and caught a rickety old omnibus headed for La Paz.

'It's orgy time tonight,' chuckled Helen as she snuggled up to Paul.

'Yes,' said Sue on his other side. 'Which of us are you going to have first, Paul?'

He grinned. 'I think I'll flip a coin.'

45

'I've got a double-header,' said Helen.

'Perhaps Paul's got a double-tailer,' said Sue, and they all laughed at the obscure dirty joke.

*

A fortnight in La Paz, gaudy capital of Bolivia. Nightclubs, where Spanish performers clicked their castanets, the aromatic haze of cigar smoke hung heavy, and a young Australian man clinked glasses of champagne with two girls.

'Cheers.'

'This is certainly better than peeling potatoes for the Sour Señora.'

'Don't talk about it,' said Sue. 'That's all part of a horrible past.'

Paul nodded. 'Yes.' He raised his glass again. 'I'm definitely a champagne man myself.'

'I never knew champagne was an aphrodisiac!'

*

The Sour Señora stood and watched as the sun went down. It was cold. The wind blew dust and grit into her face. The sun, a ball of red, dipped below the horizon. The wind moaned and it grew colder.

*

Gambling joints, where three Australians won more than they lost, then lost more than they won, then accused a croupier of cheating and got thrown out, laughing uproariously at the stir they'd caused.

'What a joke! Did you see the look on that croupier's face?'

'It certainly beats the two-up school on Anzac Day.'

*

In the heat of the day, the Sour Señora raised her eyes and looked towards the far horizon. The workers immediately slackened their pace. The sweat trickled down the back of her neck. She gazed into the distance for a long time. Her eyes were wide and unblinking.

*

Taverns, where Paul and Helen and Sue sang and danced, drank the local wine, insulted the natives and vomited into the pot plants.

'My God, that brew's strong! What do they do, put goats' piss in it?'

'I bet those pot plants die.'

'I don't think the manager appreciated it.'

'The manager can go to buggery.'

'Let's go back to the hotel. The wine hasn't ruined your sexual powers, has it, Paul?'

'Only one way to find out.'

*

I guess she has to prepare the meals herself now, thought Paul.

*

The Sour Señora, the Madam, brushed back a strand of hair as she sat over the bucket, peeling potatoes. It was late. She was very tired. The corners of her mouth were turned down.

*

I guess she's all right, he thought.

*

A bullfight, where those three gringos booed and threw cushions at

47

the local champion, then cheered and threw money to an incompetent who could not kill his bull even after three attempts.

'Some of the patrons looked as though they wanted to lynch us.'

'Yes, but they wouldn't dare. They all know the consequences.'

'That poor bloody champion! I thought he was going to break down in tears.'

'I never did like bull fights anyway.'

'Well, you probably won't get another chance to go to one here. I reckon we'll be barred after that.'

*

She's had a hard life all right, he thought.

*

The Madam, the Sour Señora, lay on her bed. She was exhausted. It was almost midnight but she could not sleep. The full moon shone through her window. The moon never changes, she thought. It is always beautiful, and it has no feelings. It is lucky.

*

I guess I've never fully appreciated the ease and comfort in my life, he thought.

*

Fancy restaurants, where the arrogant gringo troublemakers changed their orders four times, complained loudly throughout their meal, refused to pay, and were about to get involved in a fight when the police arrived.

'How did you get us out of that one, Paul?' they asked on the way back to the hotel.

'Money is a great power wielder,' he grinned.

'You've got something else that's going to wield some power before tonight's out,' said Helen. 'Come on.'

Sex and fun. Fun and sex. Fun and fun. Sex and sex.

Dissipation.

'This is tremendous,' said Sue as they relaxed on the bed.

'You certainly are a virile man,' said Helen.

Paul's eyes were closed. He nodded. His mouth smiled.

'I guess you're tired,' said Helen. 'Have a good sleep, mister virility, and we'll do it all again tomorrow.'

He did not open his eyes. 'Yes.'

'Good night, Paul,' said Helen.

'Good night, Paul,' said Sue.

''Night,' said Paul.

*

Out on the bleak Altiplano the wind was moaning. It raised swirls of dust on the barren, high Bolivian plateau. The harvest was coming to an end. Soon the workers would be leaving.

*

He got out of bed and looked through the window at the lights of sleeping La Paz. My father's rich and I have always had everything I wanted, he thought. And she's facing the start of another year of struggle on the farm. And I have beaches and parties and prawns and beer, and two girls in my bed. And the cold wind will be blowing on the desolate Altiplano. Desolate! And the sun will be shining on all the sunbathers from Melbourne to Cairns. Desolate! The Sour Señora, the girls called her. The Madam. Desolate and lonely.

*

'I'm going back,' he told them the next morning.

'What? Back home?'

'Back to the Altiplano,' he said.

Home is where the heart is.

'You're mad!'

'I'm going anyway.'

'But why, Paul? Why?'

He shrugged. How could he explain to these two university students, whose whole lives had been an adventure, a lark, strictly for the laughs? And so had his, until now.

'She needs me.'

'Who? The Sour Señora?'

The Madam, desolate and lonely, he thought.

'But what about us?'

'You don't need me.'

'But how can you go back there?'

There was no way he could explain. He just packed, slowly, aware that the last few minutes of a whole way of life were ticking away.

'How can you go back to such a…a desolate place?'

He fastened his bags and went out. He bought a horse. He mounted and set his face towards the Altiplano, the Bolivian High Plateau.

Six hours later, he worded the answer to that last question the girls had asked him. 'Desolate is a beautiful word,' he said, and urged his horse on, up onto the high Altiplano.

Disturbing Influence

Michael Whitaker was pottering about in his garden, doing nothing in particular, when those cyclists brought the bird to him that time. It was only a common house sparrow, a male, such as one sees everywhere, but it had a broken wing and a broken leg and the cyclists thought Michael might be able to nurse it back to health again.

Michael kept an aviary in his back garden, but it was visible from the main road. He sometimes thought about this fact with foreboding, fearing vandals, but none ever came. He lived in the house by himself. It was on the main road but it was a typically quiet English village, and Michael was happy enough. The house had been left him by his mother who had died some eight years ago when Michael was twenty-three, and he kept it in reasonable condition and the garden was fairly tidy.

Michael worked at the shoe factory in town six miles away, travelling by bus every day and getting home at twenty-past five, except on Fridays when he called at the bank to deposit ten pounds, which made him miss the bus and have to wait for the next one to get him home at a quarter to six. He shopped on Saturday mornings for his food, and he ate well enough. It was never sumptuous but it kept him alive and quite healthy; he got a dose of the flu in winter sometimes, but then who doesn't? The rest of the time he spent watching television, keeping the house presentable, pottering in the garden and looking after his birds.

He was not married. There had been a girl once whom he had liked, but after they had been to the cinema every Saturday night for three months, she had given him up.

It is not to be thought from all this that Michael was a morose or miserable man. He laughed at the comedies on television, he enjoyed listening to a joke at work as much as the next man, and no one who knew him hated him or feared him. True, he would never be the life and soul of the party; he was just a decent, ordinary man who got his pleasure from his birds.

They flew around in an average-sized aviary in the back garden and Michael fed and watered them and made sure they were all right every morning before he went to work. He had ten budgerigars and about the same number of zebra finches. Both breeds are very common among bird keepers: easy to feed, easy to breed, and quite hardy. Every fortnight, his copy of *Cage Birds* would come, and sometimes, in rarer moments, he thought of going in for showing them. But he didn't really like the idea. Why make an exhibition of yourself, even if it was through your birds?

Once, he remembered, he had bought a pair of Gouldian finches. They were beautiful, purple, orange and green, and Michael liked them. But they were tropical birds, hard to feed and susceptible to the unpredictable English weather. Michael kept them inside but one morning after a particularly cold night he had found them dead. Although disappointed, he had at the time felt a great sense of relief. From now on, he would stick to the good, safe old zebra finches and budgies.

Michael noticed that every Wednesday evening during the summer, bunches of cyclists would go through the village, and he knew that they were going to the local weekly race about five miles away. Later in the evening, they would struggle back, slower, quieter and obviously tired after their efforts.

Then this evening a group of them stopped outside his gate and called to him. They had found this bird on the road, hit by a car, and they wondered if he could take it and try to heal it. They had noticed his aviary in the back garden and so he must know a bit about birds. It was only a house sparrow, the commonest bird in the world, but they were a tough species and you just couldn't leave it on the road, could you?

He thanked them and said he would do what he could. They rode away, relieved to be free of the responsibility and feeling happy in the thought that they had done the right thing.

Michael Whitaker walked back into the house and put the sparrow in a cage he kept inside especially for sick birds. He didn't hold out much hope for it. And, although he did the right thing by keeping it warm and calm, somewhere deep down he hoped that the bird would die soon. He didn't want the responsibility of having to look after it for a long period of time. But he put down food and water for the bird and then went to bed.

*

When he got up the next morning, he was surprised and slightly dismayed to see that the bird was still alive. It seemed to be no better or worse. Michael had to go to work so he went through his usual routine and left. Throughout the day, he forgot about the bird and only remembered it when he walked back through the door in the evening. The bird looked up at him and seemed exactly the same. Maybe it was going to survive after all, thought Michael.

He fed his regular birds, made sure the sparrow was at least comfortable, and settled down to his evening meal. He was halfway through when there was a sudden knock on the door. He jumped. No one ever came to his place. Who could it be?

He opened the door and saw a young woman standing there, a slim, pert redhead in cycling clothes.

She didn't wait to introduce herself. 'How's the bird?' she asked. It was more like a demand.

'It's okay,' said Michael. 'Still alive. Who are you?'

'I was with the cyclists who brought it to you. But I live nearby so I've come to see it.' And with that she stepped past him and walked to the sick bird's cage.

How rude, thought Michael Whitaker. *I didn't even invite her in.*

She turned to face him. 'You thought about killing it, didn't you?' she said.

'What?'

'But you didn't. Because you're not a bad man. But it was a close thing.'

'Now look here!' said Michael. 'I didn't even invite you into the house and here you are almost accusing me of murder, even if it is only a damn sparrow.'

'And hasn't a damn sparrow got as much right to live as any other animal?' she demanded. Her hands were on her hips now and she was spoiling for a fight.

'I didn't mean it like that. And I have looked after it,' he said defensively.

'Well, it's still alive,' she said, and suddenly seemed friendlier. 'Thank you for taking care of it.' And she strode out and left.

What an impulsive woman, thought Michael. *One minute she looks as though she could punch me and the next minute she's thanking me for being kind. Well, I'll keep it warm and fed anyway.*

*

On Friday, the sparrow was still the same. When he got home from work, the girl was standing outside his back door.

'I've come to see the bird,' she said.

'Come in.'

At least I invited her in this time, he thought.

She bent and looked at the sparrow. It didn't seem to be any different. She turned to him. 'Do you think it will live?' she asked.

'I don't know,' he replied. 'Maybe it won't. But it's not as though sparrows are an endangered species.'

That was a mistake. Her hands were on her hips again.

'It's a living breathing animal,' she flared. 'It's got as much right to live as the cutest baby seal that ever bloody lived!'

'Stop swearing!' he flashed back.

'Sorry.' And she seemed suddenly smaller and prettier. 'Why don't you make a cup of tea?' And after a pause, 'As a peace offering.'

This woman will drive me crazy, he thought. *One minute she's jumping down my throat, the next minute she's apologising and wishing to sit down over a symbolic peace pipe. She's got a quick temper but if you stand up to her she'll at least quieten down and listen to you.*

'What are you going to call him?' she asked as she stood watching him make the tea.

'Who?'

'The sparrow, of course!' And left unsaid the thought, *You bloody fool.*

'I wasn't going to call it anything.'

'It isn't an it. It's a him. And he needs a name.'

'I hadn't thought about it. It's a wild animal. Wild animals don't have names.'

'What about Augustine?' she said.

'Augustine?'

'Yes. After Saint Augustine.' She stepped a little closer to him. 'You know his famous quotation, don't you?' It was a statement more than a question.

'Quotation? No.'

'Give me chastity and constancy,' she said, 'but not yet.' And leaned slightly toward him.

'Your cup of tea is ready,' he said. 'Sit down.'

They faced each other over the table.

'You've not even asked me my name,' she said.

'Well, what is it?'

'Pat Fox. People call me the Red Fox. On account of my hair, you know. Sometimes it just gets shortened to Red.'

'Well, mine's Michael Whitaker.'

'I know.'

'How did you know?'

'It's written on your letter box.'

'Oh. Ah yes, so it is.' And he felt foolish and dull and didn't know what to say next.

'I don't live very far away,' she said eventually. 'I live in the village.'

'Do you? Where?'

'On Phoenix Street.'

'Oh yes, I know where that is,' he said.

'Number five. Third house on the left. I live by myself. No pets. No dogs to frighten away visitors,' she said, looking at him. 'And no birds to worry about.' She finished her drink and stood up again. 'Got to go. I want to do some training before it gets dark. 'Bye.'

Michael chuckled to himself when she was gone. *The Red Fox. And Augustine. What unusual names. Well, at least there's no danger of getting them mixed up with anybody else.*

*

The next day being Saturday, Michael did his weekly shopping and in the afternoon went to see a film in town. He came home on the bus and was surprised to find her waiting for him at the bus stop.

'Augustine is starting to worry me,' she said.

You're not the only one who's worried, he thought. *It will be all over the village if anybody sees me walking with a girl.*

'Why is it worrying you?' he forced himself to say as they entered his house.

She went to the sparrow, Augustine, and seemed to examine it closely. 'I'm worried if it will ever breed,' she said.

'Don't see why not. If it recovers.'

'Do birds have testosterone?'

'I don't know. I guess they must have some sort of bird equivalent.'

She twisted her lips into a wry smile. 'There's been millions of songs written in celebration of male testosterone. And not a few about female hormones.' She grinned openly, showing her white teeth.

Michael looked woodenly at the sparrow. 'Well, first it's got to get better. And I've done what I can.'

She looked at him. 'Have you?' Then she was gone.

She's a disturbing influence, that girl, he thought. *But I never noticed before how white her teeth are.*

*

On the Sunday, he worked in his garden a little, cleaned his regular birds, vacuumed the house and watched a bit of television. She didn't come at all that day and he found himself wondering why. He tended the sick sparrow and seemed to think that it was improving slightly. *But I'm not sure*, he thought. *Maybe that's just my imagination.* And he smiled to himself, just a little. Imagination was a thing he seldom associated with himself.

*

On the Monday, he went to work as normal, but during the day he seemed preoccupied. He found himself worrying about whether she would turn up that evening to enquire about Augustine. And he wondered why she hadn't come the day before.

When he got home, there she was! But it was another shock. She was inside his house and already making him a cup of tea.

'What are you doing breaking into my house!?' he demanded.

'I didn't break in. I found your spare key and let myself in. I've only been here a couple of minutes.'

'How did you know where I keep the spare key?'

'It was under the brick near the back door. A man like you would always use a conventional place like that.'

A man like you? he thought, and felt his heart jump a little. *This woman is a disturbing influence. She's annoying, she's brash, she's downright cheeky.* Then he thought, *But she's obviously honest and generous. She could have stolen anything and yet here she is making me a drink.*

'How's the bird?' he asked.

'The bird? Don't you mean Augustine? He's got a name, you know.'

'Well, how the bloody hell is he?'

'Now *you're* swearing.'

Michael didn't so much give an exasperated sigh as just exhale loudly.

'Augustine looks a bit sicker, I think,' she said as she brought the mugs of tea to the table.

She sat down opposite him. 'Perhaps he's going to die.'

He bowed his head, not in grief but in embarrassment. He still found it hard to look her straight in the eye, especially at close quarters.

'Poor old Augustine,' she said cryptically.

They sat in silence for a little while. Michael was wondering what to say next.

'Where were you yesterday?' he asked eventually.

'It was race day and then we all went riding after that. When I got back, I was tired and it was dark. I thought about coming round but figured you might be in bed by then.' She paused slightly. 'Wouldn't want to disturb you in bed.'

She turned, looking slightly flushed, and seemed to examine the bird. 'Did you miss me?' she asked in a small high-pitched voice.

'Well, I wondered where you'd got to. I thought perhaps you'd lost interest in Augustine.'

'Oh no,' she said. 'But I do have a life of my own to live, you know.' She turned to face him again across the table and that awkward silence descended once more.

'Do you ever wonder what you'll be like in the next life?'

'The next life?' he retorted. 'What are you talking about?'

'The Buddhists believe in reincarnation. Seems to make a lot of sense to me.'

'I've never…'

'You're not going to give me that old chestnut about all men being born equal, are you?' she said. 'That's rubbish. You've only got to think about that for a second to see how ridiculous it is.'

'I have to admit…'

'It's how you live in this life that determines what circumstances you get born into in the next life,' she said. 'That sounds logical to me.'

'Are you a Buddhist?'

'No. But I think a lot of their ideas make sense.'

'What about animals? Do they get reincarnated?'

'I don't know,' she said. 'I don't know about them. I hope so. They're living creatures after all. But I'm no expert. I just think it's interesting.'

She got up, ready to go. 'I'm tired after my big ride yesterday. I'll see you tomorrow.'

She paused at the door. 'It's how you live in this life, Michael,' she said.

And suddenly he found himself staring at the closed door.

*

At work the next day, Michael had a rough time. He was assigned a hard job and he didn't do it very well. He found it hard to concentrate. The boss asked him a couple of times what was the matter and Michael didn't know the answer.

By the time he got home, he was in a ratty mood. The Red Fox wasn't there and he found himself relieved and disappointed at the same time. *Perhaps she's gone out training,* he thought. *She's got a life of her own.* Then, *Can't you think of anything more original to say to yourself than that?* But it was probably true after all, because when she did turn up a while later, she was in her cycling gear and had obviously been out riding.

Michael was just finishing his meal when she knocked and walked straight in.

'How's Augustine?'

'He's okay, I guess,' said Michael morosely.

She understood his mood in an instant. 'How are you?' she said, almost gently.

'All right.'

'I'll make a cup of tea.'

A cup of tea, the answer to everything, he thought. Then, *pull yourself together, man.*

They sat across the table from each other, silently drinking the tea.

Michael made an effort to be cordial. 'How was your ride?'

'Fine,' she replied. 'I'm getting fitter.'

'Do you win many races?'

She gave a short laugh. 'No. I'm no champion. But I enjoy it. I get out, see a few different places, and every ride is a little adventure.'

'Hm.' He didn't know what to say after that.

They sat for a while longer and she took a couple of deep breaths and seemed to brace herself.

'When are you going to start having adventures, Michael?'

'What? What do you mean?'

'You've got a steady job, you own the house, you don't have to worry where your next meal is coming from. When are you going to adventure on life?'

'What are you talking about?'

'Life is either a great adventure or nothing. Helen Keller said that.'

The rattiness had not left Michael. 'You're very smart on the quotes, aren't you?' he said sarcastically.

She leapt up. 'And if somebody else can express it better than I can, what's wrong with that? Wake up to yourself, Michael! Your life is too comfortable. It's too dull. You don't do anything daring at all. This bird is the most interesting thing that's ever happened to you!' She was at full tilt now and nothing was going to stop her. 'Is that how you want to live all the time? Get off your lazy arse and do something with your life!'

But Michael's rough day exploded too. 'Stop swearing in my house! Who do you think you are? You come in here uninvited, you break into my house, you suggest a stupid name for a common sparrow, and now you're trying to tell me how to live! Well, I don't want your advice!'

'Yes, you do! Haven't you ever loved anything, Michael?' And in a smaller voice, 'Haven't you ever loved any*one*?'

But he wasn't listening. 'I think you've outstayed your welcome here. The bird will live or die whether you come or not.'

'I'm going,' and the tears hung on her eyelashes. 'I'm going,' and she rushed out.

Michael Whitaker sat down and took a few deep breaths. *So she was gone. And,* he thought, *she would never come back. He could slouch back down into his old safe routine again. No arguments, no fights, no discussions about philosophy or birds or cycling or anything.* And he realised he was going to miss her. The Red Fox. A quirky name for a pretty girl, almost as silly as Augustine for a common house sparrow.

He moved and washed the two teacups, and his stomach felt heavy. He felt lonely and miserable. *It's just been a rough day*, he thought. *One of those days.*

He thought of how many of 'those days' stretched out in front of him: going to work in his safe job, coming home to his safe house, and living a safe and dull life. He sat thinking. The Red Fox had said that life is either a great adventure or nothing. And he thought of her ideas about the Buddhists and reincarnation.

If reincarnation is the way things are, he thought, *I wonder what I will be like in the next life?* And immediately the answer came to him. *It depends how you live in this life.*

He realised how churlish he had been towards her. And he knew what he must do about it. Now, without hesitation.

He turned to the bird, Augustine the sparrow. It seemed weaker than before and its eyes betrayed its suffering. He found himself talking to it. 'The Buddhists believe in reincarnation,' he said. 'The Red Fox taught me that. I hope that in the next life you will be a beautiful bird in a warm place, where there is plenty of food and where there are no predators and no humans.'

He went into his room and put on his coat, ready to walk around to Phoenix Street. To the third house on the left, where there were no dogs to frighten away visitors and no birds to worry about. As he came out, he looked again at the sparrow. It looked back at him and watched him as he walked out the door.

Augustine the sparrow lay there for a long time after Michael Whitaker was gone. It was warm there; it had food and water and it was safe inside its cage where no predators could get it. And now there were no humans.

The bird continued to look at the closed door. Then its head dropped and it was dead.

Forgiven

I shouldn't be in here. They got the wrong man. I never did it. It was that bastard Foster. He got on the drugs and killed the girl. He shouldn't have even been driving; his licence had been suspended and he'd stolen the car. Only trouble is, he's in with the wrong crowd. And I mean 'the wrong crowd'! Not only gangsters, but gangsters who are in with the police. This is a corrupt town.

Because I look a bit like Foster and I sometimes speak to him, the cops came very early one morning and took me away. It was no good protesting. The cops knew I was innocent, the judge knew I was innocent, but the gangsters had the money for bribes. And if the bribes didn't work, they had the muscle to persuade them. One of the jurors turned up with a broken arm and a black eye, and everyone got the message. I was the fall guy, and Foster walked free, and everyone was happy except me and the mother of the dead girl.

Well, I'm not staying in here for twenty years. I've got an escape plan. I'm working on it. In two weeks, I'll be out.

Three weeks later

I'm sitting in my comfortable home, watching TV and sipping a drink and feeling quite secure. And it may surprise you when I say that my escape didn't go to plan.

There I was, sitting in my cell doing nothing, when the guard came and unlocked my door and said, 'Off you go.' Just like that!

I said, 'What's going on?'

He smiled and said, 'I'm the same as everybody else in this town, mate. I'm in the pay of the gang. And they've decided that you're innocent after all. Which automatically means that the judge has decided you're innocent. Now get going before they change their minds!'

Well, I didn't need telling twice. So I came home and wondered what was going to happen next. Was I being set up for something more sinister? I didn't want to get mixed up with the gang but I was curious as to what had made them change their mind.

Then last night it happened. The head gangster came to see me. We sat down and he explained.

'The mother of the girl who was killed,' he said, 'went to see Foster. You know her of course. She knew he was really the guilty one. She tried to persuade Foster to give himself up and confess. But appealing to Foster's conscience is a lost cause. He told her to get out. So she came to me and persuaded me that Foster should be behind bars, not you.'

'How did she manage to persuade you?' I asked.

I swear to you that this hard-bitten gangster even blushed slightly.

'She's an attractive woman,' he said. 'And I'm a normal red-blooded guy.' He took a deep breath. 'Anyway, I arranged it, and here you are. And Foster's in jail where he should be.'

So justice has been done after all, in its strange way. And of course I know the woman. And it's good I'm free again to do my work with the people of the town.

I was able to conduct the sacrament on Sunday as usual, and afterwards the woman and I spent some time together.

'Can you forgive Foster for what he did?' she asked.

I screwed my face. 'That's hard,' I said. 'But it's my job to forgive.'

'Can you forgive me?' she said.

'Oh yes,' I said. 'I forgive you readily.'

Then together we said a prayer for the salvation of Foster's soul. And I spent some time alone, struggling to find in my own soul a spirit of forgiveness for that man.

She came to me as I wept for the memory of the girl, and raised me from where I knelt. 'Come,' she said. 'Come with me.'

It was a mellow summer Sunday evening, the sun shone low through the trees, and the world was quiet.

And later she whispered to me, 'Nothing can replace our lost daughter. But I feel that already we may be having another child.'

How To Become a Champion

All right, I did wrong, I admit it. I couldn't very well deny it, could I, standing in the middle of the girls' playground where we boys weren't allowed. I only wanted to chat with Jessica Rowley, which I was doing quite innocently. But I didn't notice Mr Bradley coming up behind me.

'Jackson!' he barked. 'You know you're not allowed here! Come with me!' And he grabbed me by the scruff of the neck and marched me up to his office.

I didn't like that. Being caught was one thing. Being marched off in front of everyone bruised my fifteen-year-old pride. My resentful feelings flared.

In his office, he gave me a stern lecture. That was no more than I expected, and perhaps a detention or something like that.

But then he got his cane and said, 'Bend over.'

Now six strokes of the cane are painful. I gritted my teeth and forced myself not to cry. But he wasn't finished. He marched me out to the field and made me run six laps at full effort, with everyone looking on. It was nothing short of sadistic.

I got home and I did what every schoolboy does. I breathed revenge. I swore that when I got big and strong enough, after I'd left school, I would come back and give that bastard six of the best of his own and see how he liked it. I'm not trying to say I didn't deserve punishment: I knew I'd done wrong. I'm just saying the punishment was excessive for the offence, and I have always hated injustice.

Lots of schoolboys have had similar experiences. And they get over it. Go to university, get a job, get involved with other things. And forget the whole thing, the whole injustice of it. Not me. I never forgot it. I intended getting my own back.

A year later, I had left school but I hadn't forgotten the bastard Bradley. But I wasn't strong enough to get my revenge yet.

I started training hard. Ran, cycled, went to physical fitness classes, tried karate and then took up boxing. I almost seemed to enjoy getting hit. It helped to fuel my hatred of the man who had wronged me.

I took part in boxing matches and had a fair amount of success. I gained a reputation as a hard man. The time was coming when I would wreak my revenge on Bradley.

I had an important fight coming up for the area championship, and I judged that after that, while I was still fit and hard, I would visit my old nemesis and even the scores.

In addition to the actual boxing training, I used to go to the weights room and work out in order to get stronger. And about a week before my big fight, I noticed this attractive girl there and went to talk to her.

'I'm sure I've seen you before,' I said.

She looked at me. 'How corny,' she said. 'But I think I do know you. Aren't you Steve Jackson?'

'Yes. And you are…?'

'Jessica Rowley. Remember me from school?'

Well, how she had changed! Grown up! Nice. Oh yes, very nice.

Now I have been a hard man, I admit, somewhat self-absorbed, and I had been with a few women. But after the training session I couldn't wait to talk to her.

'Take care in the big fight,' she said as we sat over coffee. 'I don't want you getting too hurt.'

'Will you come?'

'Yes. I'll come and be cheering for you.'

Well, if ever I needed a boost, this was it. I couldn't lose the fight now. I just couldn't! Not with her cheering for me!

I saw her again, just twenty-four hours before the fight, and she repeated her concerns.

'Don't worry,' I said. 'I'll be fighting for you.'

Then we kissed and held each other – and that was all!

'Get a good night's sleep,' she said with a twinkle in her eye. 'Save your strength for tomorrow.'

I have never felt so elated going into the ring. I'm sure my opponent felt the vibes, because he seemed intimidated from the start. He was a skilful boxer but I concentrated hard and beat him on points.

He shook my hand like a gentleman afterwards and said, 'You have a lot of potential. I think you can go far. Good luck!'

But I had only one thing on my mind. Jessica!

She came to my dressing room after I had changed.

'Let's celebrate,' she said, and she had that twinkle in her eye again.

It is no exaggeration to say that my boxing career moved up to a new level after that. And I had no illusions what had caused it. There seemed to be two opposing motivations: one was my love for Jess, which had developed strongly and smoothly, and the other was still my simmering resentment of the injustice I had suffered at the hands of Mr Bradley. There was still that score to settle.

But there was another thing to do first. Having won the area championship, I was now a contender for the state championship and I wanted my full concentration on that. My manager organised a title fight for three months ahead with Scott Denman, the reigning state champ, and I wisely thought I would keep Bradley on the back burner during that time. I fully realised that my simmering resentment of that man was helping me be more aggressive in the ring.

'You're an angry young man,' said Jess to me one day. 'You have a chip on your shoulder.' She snuggled up to me. 'What is it?'

It was time I shared more of my life with her. 'It goes back to that old schoolteacher of mine,' I said. 'You've probably forgotten the incident, but I never have.' And I recounted the occasion of my humiliation at the hands of Mr Bradley. 'He was a ratbag and a bastard,' I said. 'And I still hate him. That's what makes me angry.'

And while I was raving on, I failed to notice that she was staring at me without blinking.

'He's my uncle,' she said quietly.

'What?'

'You heard me. He's my uncle. I never mentioned it at school because I didn't want people to think I was privileged. And he's a good man.' She prepared to get out of the car. 'It's time you grew up!' she hissed, and slammed the door and stalked off.

I thumped the steering wheel until my hand hurt. Bastard! Bastard! Bastard! Not only had the man humiliated me at school he was now the cause of me losing my girlfriend. Bastard!

I slammed the car into gear and roared off to the gym. I was going to thump the hell out of that punchbag. But then the red and blue lights flashed behind me and suddenly I was standing at the side of the road being booked for speeding. Two days later, I had been fined a substantial amount and had my licence suspended for three months.

Bastard! Bastard!

It made me angrier than ever, but it was a blessing in disguise. Because I now had to run the four kilometres to the gym every day, and run back when I had finished my training. It gave me extra stamina, granted, but every evening when I arrived home, exhausted and drenched either from sweat or the rain, I cursed the man who had caused me all these troubles. A chip on my shoulder? Yes. And Denman, my opponent in the state championships, was going to feel the brunt of it.

No car, no girlfriend, and still a score to settle with that man. How I hated him!

Came the big night and my trainer spoke to me. 'It's often a ploy,' he said, 'for trainers to deliberately annoy their man before a fight so that he'll vent his anger on his opponent. I don't think I need to do that with you. Whatever it is that's eating you, get out there and thump it into Denman. You'll need it, because he's good.'

What!? I almost hit my trainer then. To tell me that my opponent was good was implying that he might beat me. Well, I'd show him! I'd show everybody! I'd show my trainer, I'd show Denman, I'd show Jessica, I'd show Bradley. I'd show the lot of them who they were dealing with!

I almost ran out to the ring to get started.

Well, of course in my more reasonable moments, I knew that Denman was good. You don't get to be state champion if you're not good. But he had no chance that night. I'm not going to be a bore and describe the fight blow by blow; suffice to say that I landed a hell of a lot more blows than he did. And when the referee stopped the fight in my favour after seven rounds, I was still ready to hit some more.

But now I was state champion!

Now, a boxing match is a hard thing. They never show you the scenes in the dressing rooms immediately after a bout, but I can tell you now it's not pretty. Even though I had won convincingly, I still collapsed on the massage table and it took me a while to come round properly.

'It worked,' said my trainer.

'What?'

'I annoyed you after all, didn't I?'

Well, of course he'd annoyed me, and now I saw that it had been deliberate all along. 'You old scoundrel,' I said, and grinned.

'Someone to see you,' he said.

And who should walk in but Jess – and Mr Bradley himself! He seemed smaller than I remembered.

'I'm sorry,' said Jess. 'I'm sorry. It was me who needed to grow up too. I want to come back to you.'

As we hugged, I saw Mr Bradley. He looked as though he wanted to say something.

'Jackson,' he said. 'You've cost me a lot of money tonight.'

'How come?'

'I bet a good amount on the other fellow. And I've lost it.'

I chuckled to myself then. So this was my revenge. No need to slap him now, possibly get arrested for assault, and lose Jess forever.

But he hadn't finished. 'I always thought you were a bit of a chump,' he said. 'But now I see you're a champ. I'm sorry – and congratulations.' And he held out his hand to be shaken.

I figured him saying he was sorry was his way of apologising for the injustice of all those years ago. We were even at last.

Suddenly another man walked into the room. It was a reporter. 'Mr Jackson,' he said. 'Congratulations on being the new state champion. To what do you owe your success?'

I grinned as I reached to shake Mr Bradley's hand. 'I guess I owe it all to this man,' I said.

There's more than one way to be a champion!

I Got Feelings Too, Doc

Well, Doc, I guess you're wondering why I addressed this note to you and not to the police or whoever finds me. I guess it's because perhaps you're the only person I know who might understand. And even then I'm not sure. But I got to try and explain to somebody, Doc, before I go.

I suppose you're wondering if it's suicide, Doc. Well, it is. I'm doing myself in. When I've finished this, I'm going to take all them pills you gave me about six weeks ago. And I suppose you're wondering why. Well, this is to try and tell you.

It all really started when I came here on that big fencing job on the Barker property. I done a good job there. I was a good fencer in them days. Then when Plummers' job came up, then the Watsons' after that, I thought I might settle down here and try to make a go of a little business. I always did like this area.

Well, of course, Doc, you know how I got going regular with Jenny Simpson. I don't have to spell it out for you. You seen it all. But perhaps you didn't know that she thought she'd make me stop drinking once we was married. I know I'm a drinker and a ratbag but I tried to be good to her and I reckon we was happy. Or at least I was happy, and because I was happy I thought she was happy too. Only natural, ain't it? Well, she did try and stop me drinking, but I told her not to be a wowser and a spoilsport and after a bit she left it alone.

As I said, we was happy, or I was. My job took me away for a fair bit and I got to seeing some of the countryside. A change of scenery, see. I guess I never thought of her being stuck in a little town like this. She'd grown up here and she knew everybody, so I thought she'd be okay while I was gone on the job. It gave me a chance to have a drink and a yarn with the boys, too. A man needs that. Or so I thought.

Anyway, we was working on that new property up near Nimmabooka. You know the one I mean. There was four of us for a start but then one day the boss brought another fellow and said he'd be working with us too. This new guy's name was Ted Donlington. Seemed he drifted around picking up jobs wherever he could. Well, we tested him out at first, as you do, gave him the hardest jobs to see what he was made of, and it turns out he's a real good worker. Knew how to do fencing, all right. And he was a good bloke too. Fitted in real well. When we went into town, he drank as good as the rest of us, but he knew when to stop. I respected him for that. You know me, Doc, I usually lay meself out after a few jars but Ted got me into the car and drove us all back. I'd been pulled up by the local cop for drink driving before so I appreciated him doing that.

Next morning, we were all a bit slow, Ted included, but we laughed it off as you do in the bush and we got on with the job. I reckon he was the best fencer out of the lot of us, me included. But he didn't try and make himself look special or anything, just got on with the job, and he was always cheery and ready with a joke.

When we finished the job, I asked him where he was heading for next, and he said he didn't know. So I told him he could come and stay with us if he liked, 'cos we'd be back home in a couple of days, and then he could decide what he wanted to do next. He was one of those blokes you take a liking to straight away, Doc. He was everything I would like to have been – and could have been if I'd had a bit more brains and courage.

I drove him back into town and brought him home. He settled in well but said he'd only be staying a few days. Had to move on, he said, find another job, keep moving.

'Don't you ever want to settle down?' I asked.

He glanced at Jenny – I'm sure he did – and said, 'Well, maybe one day. Maybe one day.'

'It must be romantic moving around like you do,' says Jenny.

'Yeah,' he said, and laughed a bit. 'It's not bad. You get used to it.'

'I've never been nowhere,' she says.

'You were born here,' I says. 'You know everybody. What's the matter with you!'

Anyway, we went to bed and I was tired and went to sleep straight away.

When I gets up in the morning – well, you know, Doc, I don't have to tell you. She'd gone, and so had he. Gone. Together. And I should of seen it coming.

Well, I got feelings too, Doc, and suddenly I seen what a bastard I'd been for neglecting her and all. Going up the country and leaving her here feeling lonely all the time. I tell you, I felt lower than a snake's belly.

But he'd gone and taken her with him, on to their gypsy life. Leaving me here, like a fool.

*

All that was two years ago, Doc. Two years of being laughed at, sometimes not even behind my back. You know how my business has gone down. At first I thought she'd come back. That's why I stayed on, so that if she ever wanted me she'd know where to find me. But now I realise she's not coming back. And I've had enough.

You see, I got feelings too, Doc. Oh, I know they all say I'm a drunkard and a bum. I know what they say, and I know what you say too, Doc. It's easy for you because you're not involved. Move away, you say. Forget it all, start a new life. But it ain't that easy, Doc. This is where she knows where to find me, dead or alive, even if it's in fifty years' time. You see, Doc, you see – I loved her too!

*

I just took them pills you gave me, Doc. Took them all in one go. It's taken me six weeks to work up the courage. And what finally made me?

I don't know. Guess it's just pressure that builds up, keeps building up so that it's no one particular thing that makes you finally do it in the end. Building up over two years. I guess that's it.

Well, I've taken the pills, Doc, so I reckon there ain't much time left. I hereby make out my last will and testament and leave it all to you, Doc. It's only a few dollars. I want you to spend it on a good clear headstone so she won't have no trouble finding me if she ever comes back.

Starting to feel a bit drowsy now, Doc, but I think I've said it all. They'll all remember me as the town drunk, but there was a reason wasn't there.

Feeling drowsy. Reckon this is it. Drowsy now. Goodbye, Doc, hope you understand it all. Yo see I got feelins too Doc I got f

Jacob's Street

Lots of people get it wrong. They call it Jacobs Street. We put them right straight away. It's Jacob's Street. With an apostrophe and all. As in street belonging to Jacob. Inga taught me that. About apostrophes, I mean. It's easy once you get the hang of it. Before that our street didn't have a real name. We just called it East Street because it ran East. In a town of only four hundred souls, not all of them bright as the morning star, there ain't many streets. Or lanes. Whatever.

There's only eight houses on it even now. I counted up once, fourteen people, not counting old Tom Bellow who visits Amy Gee almost every night. But he don't live here so he don't count.

People think we're poor because it ain't got bitumen and kerbs and all that stuff. Well, we don't want it, because then other people would want to live here, and we're happy with just our eight houses, and only Inga and me know the real story behind its name. Me and Inga aren't married or nothing – well, not yet – but we're very good friends and I'll let your imagination do the rest.

Well, we weren't even 'very good friends' when it all started. Oh, we lived next door to each other and all, but her husband had only just left her and she had three kids to suddenly bring up on her own, so I tried to help her. Mowed her lawn for her, gave her a few vegies from my garden, stuff like that. She was grateful but said she didn't want to feel too beholden to me, and after I looked up what that fancy word meant I could see her point. She probably thought I was trying to get on to her with all this generosity stuff. Well, maybe. She's a not bad-looker even after three kids, and she's definitely cleverer than me, or anybody else in the street for that matter.

She comes from Denmark originally and English ain't her first language, which shows just how smart she is. Hell, she knows it better than me now. And she didn't leave school till she was seventeen. That must be a record in our town.

Anyways, me and Inga was becoming friends because I was being nice to her, as I told you. It wasn't real hard work. I've got a regular job which manages to pay the rent and I don't drink very much, so I usually have a bit left over every pay, and I was wondering how I could help her with her rent because that ratbag of a husband had upped and gone and she didn't have much money. I couldn't just go around and plonk money on her table and I was getting a bit worried because I didn't want to see her get evicted, not with her living next door and being such a good-looker and our relationship getting better all the time. There's a word for you. Relationship. She taught me that one too.

So home I comes from work this particular evening and there's a note in the letter box demanding – demanding! – that I attend a meeting in Clyde Westerman's house at number six. Clyde's got the biggest house in the street, not that that's saying much, but at least he's got a big lounge with a carpet in it, even.

Well, that put me in a good mood straight away and I'm not being sarcastic because within a couple of minutes there's Inga knocking on my door and asking if I've got a letter just like she has. It was the first time she had come round to my place like that, which showed that she regarded me as a friend to confide in. So I was happy and she stayed and had a cup of tea with me but had to get back to the kids pretty quick. She was worried about what to do with them until we looked closer at the letter and it said everyone in the street must attend, so we figured that included the kids too.

So when the time came, off we toddles just like a regular family and everything, Inga with the youngest one, Louise, still a babe in arms, me leading the toddler Steven, and Anna, six, skipping along beside us. Inga had told her that this was an important meeting and she had to be quiet, and Anna's a good kid anyways.

We gets to Clyde's and most of the other folk are there already, but there's this one guy who nobody knows and it turns out that he's the one who's called the meeting. Says his name is Jacob Holstein, and when we're ready to listen he gets going and what a shock! Turns out he's bought all eight houses in the damned street. All eight! Just like that. Must have piles of money and also plenty of influence because just about every house in the whole town is owned by the big grocery factory that employs everyone, including me. But he's now the owner of the whole street.

Uh oh, here it comes, I thought, he's going to increase the rent and get us all thrown out and then bulldoze the houses down and build units or something like that. But I couldn't of been wronger. Says he's going to halve the rents! Halve them! Is he crazy? Says he's got plenty of money and he can afford it and he thinks the grocery factory charges too much rent anyway.

So Inga speaks up. She's the smartest of us all, which means she ain't gonna get conned this easy. 'What's the catch?' she says.

'No catch,' says this man. 'Just a couple of conditions.'

I saw a twisted smile come to Inga's lips – God, she looked pretty when she did that! – and I knew what was on her mind. Here comes the sting, she was thinking. But it was a very mild sting if that.

'Two conditions,' he said. 'One, that you don't tell anybody else in the town, because then they'll get jealous and we all know what problems that can cause. And two, that you pay into this bank account, I'll give you the number, and all you have to do is go to the bank every month and pay in your money. Or you can do it on the computer if you want.'

Well, not many of us around here have got a computer, not on this street anyway, but we let that slide.

'Mister Holstein,' says Inga, 'I don't want to sound ungrateful or even cynical, but this sort of thing just doesn't happen. There's got to be a catch.'

'I told you, there's no catch,' he says. 'Look, I'm not a young man and I have no one to leave my fortune to. If I can do a bit of good in this world, then this is how I'm doing it before it's too late. Simple as that.'

And he made us take an oath that we wouldn't tell anyone else, which we all took willingly, and then he gave us the number of this bank account which we had to pay our rent into. By this time, we'd shared a coffee or tea and some snacks and it seems he's just a regular guy like anybody else, only with lots of money. We ended up calling him Jacob because he asked us to, not Mister Holstein or anything formal like that.

As me and Inga and the kids walked home, there was only one thing to talk about. Inga was still wary. So was I as far as that goes.

But it seemed that Jacob Holstein was as good as his word. No bulldozers came along, nothing unusual happened, and when we went into the city to pay our rent it was as straightforward as buying a bar of chocolate. Or a cup of coffee and a nice sandwich, which is what me and Inga did because we all went in my car, baby Louise asleep in the back, toddler Steven falling asleep, and six-year-old Anna fascinated by what she saw out of the window. And best of all, Inga kissed me when we got home and said thank you for the ride, it was very sweet of you. I went to bed a happy man that night, I can tell you.

Well, only having to pay half as much rent as before certainly made life a lot easier. But it brought its worries too. Drongo Sullivan drinks a bit too much sometimes and I was concerned he might blab about our secret.

I called him into my house one day and also asked Clyde Westerman and Inga herself to be there. Then I got a razor blade, just nicked the end of my little finger, Clyde and Inga both did the same, and then we made Drongo do it too, and we mixed our blood and made him close his eyes and take a solemn oath on his dear old Irish mother's deathbed not to say anything about our new arrangement. That did it. Drongo was as white as a sheet when we'd finished but he's as superstitious as they come and I figured we were safe now.

Inga and I were getting along real well. Sometimes she'd ask me to take care of the kids when she went shopping, and I enjoyed that, but I could see when she came back that she'd not bought too much, not with three children to feed, and I knew she was still doing it tough. All these allowances that the government give you don't go far. I was seriously thinking of asking her to marry me. I knew she had to get a divorce first – well, that happens, half the town are on their second or third marriage so that didn't worry me. And the kids were a ready-made family, not that I had any objections to us having some of our own, but I was thinking too far ahead because it didn't turn out to be that simple.

Anna, the six-year-old girl, came into my garden sometimes just to play. I guess it was a break from the two younger ones for her, and Inga knew about it and didn't mind, which I thought was another good sign that she trusted me. But suddenly I heard a scream and there's Anna standing in the backyard going ballistic and when I gets to her she's crying and can't say anything but she points and there's a bloody snake nearby, and I ask her has it bitten her and she nods and nods and nods, because she's crying too much to say anything, so I grabs her in my arms and bundles her in the car and races out without even telling Inga and into the city where there's a hospital and straight into emergency without stopping and yelling this girl's been bitten by a snake, this girl's been bitten by a snake! They all come rushing and want to know what sort of snake it was and I says a brown snake, they can be deadly especially to a child, and they rush her into emergency and tell me they'll do everything they can.

Then they say I can't do anything now for a while, it's up to the medical team, so I figure I'd better go back and tell Inga, seeing as neither of us has got a phone, we're not that rich, so back I goes and tells her and she just about faints at my feet but we all get in the car, toddler and baby and all and head back to the hospital. I must say they were very good, assuring us that everything is being done and giving us cups of tea, not that we felt like drinking it, but they looked after Steven and baby Louise.

I held Inga tight and would have loved that if it had been a normal night but this wasn't anything like normal so those sort of thoughts weren't around and I just held her and tried to comfort her but I felt as guilty as hell because it had happened in my yard and I should have been keeping a closer eye on her.

That was the most traumatic night of my life. Traumatic, that's another word Inga's taught me. But it fits perfectly. Inga eventually fell asleep in my arms, which as I said was great in itself, but I couldn't sleep and it was past midnight when the doctor came out and said she's going to be all right. Well, look, I'm a big strong guy and I don't take no nonsense from nobody but I blubbered like a little baby then. That woke Inga up and I was able to tell her that her daughter was going to live. So she held me tighter than ever and we both blubbed for a bit, but then Inga said can we see her and they said yes but don't get her excited, she's still weak and will need to sleep.

Now, I suppose you're wondering what all this has got to do with our street being called Jacob's Street. Well, I'm coming to that, because it's one thing to have someone's life saved in the hospital but it's another thing to have to pay for it. Things like that come to a lot of money. Inga couldn't pay it and it wasn't her place to either, it was my responsibility because it had happened on my property so I insisted on paying, but when I got the bill I knew I was in trouble.

I'd got a bit saved up but it wasn't enough. I asked the hospital if I could pay it in instalments and they said, well, it's very irregular but they could make arrangements. For weeks I scrimped and saved, and it was hard, because I'd grown used to buying the occasional snack to share with Inga and the kids and now I couldn't do that any more. Inga was nice to me and that was great, Anna was fully recovered, and it seemed I was the only one left with a problem out of the whole thing.

It was getting to be impossible and to my way of thinking there was only one thing to do. I would have to miss out on paying the rent for a month. Once I'd paid off the hospital, I could catch up, and I would explain that when the overdue notice came. But it never did.

No overdue notice. Well, I went another month without paying the rent and at last that got the hospital paid off. But still no overdue rent notice.

Only one person to take this problem to. My next-door neighbour, my best friend, the lovely girl who'd totally forgiven me for Anna's snakebite, who'd got herself the official divorce and who even occasionally brought a snack over to me now that I was the poor one. Inga, good trusty level-headed intelligent beautiful Inga.

'It's a problem,' she said. 'Maybe they're sending it to the wrong address.'

But quiet enquiries revealed that no one was overdue in their rent and no one had received any sort of notice. I was worried that one day out of the blue the bailiffs would be at my door throwing me out and not believing me when I said I'd never had any warning.

'What we'll do,' said Inga, 'is go into the city and find out about this bank account and why they're not sending out overdue notices.'

Well, I'm not very good at that sort of thing and besides I had a job of work to do, but Inga went in and when she came back she looked exhausted.

I made her a cup of tea and we sat in the kitchen.

'It took a lot of digging and I still don't have the full story,' she said. 'But we're paying our rents into a registered charity all the time.'

'How do you mean?'

'It's a charity that helps victims of crime. Our combined rents from all eight houses go into it, month after month. They're classed as donations. So if you don't pay, it's not a legally binding thing that they can nail you for.'

'Why would that guy, that Jacob Holstein, have done that?'

'That's what I don't know. I want to go in again on Thursday and try to find out. Can you get the day off and come with me?'

Yes, of course I could, so off we went. Anna was in school, Steven the toddler was now in kindergarten, so we only had little Louise to worry about and I held her most of the time while Inga made further investigations. That's how it should have been anyway; as I said, she's smart and I wouldn't have known what to do. But I will say that I'm good with the kids and Louise was no problem.

It was a long day. She had to chase between two or three offices, which we did in the car, but by the time we'd finished, she had a knowing smile on her face – God, she looked nice when she did that! – and she said she'd tell me the whole story after we'd picked up the kids and got home.

We put the kids to bed after the evening meal and then we sat down and she told me what she'd learnt.

'For a start,' she said, 'his name wasn't Jacob Holstein. He made that up because – would you believe – he was a criminal. Apparently he'd been a big-time business man, which is where he got his money, but one day he killed somebody in a hit-and-run accident. And no one knew it was him until, after he'd been to see us, he walked into a police station and confessed. I guess he told us a different name so that we wouldn't recognise him in the papers when his trial came up. He was put in jail and died not long afterwards. The ownership of our houses is in a trust he set up, and they can't increase our rents for the next twenty years. The reason he bought our houses and got us to pay our money into that account for the victims of crime was his way of making amends. An atonement, if you like.'

'A what?'

'An atonement. It means trying to make up for what you've done wrong. Like you with Anna, going without, just to pay the hospital bill because you felt responsible and it was your place to pay the debt.' She looked me in the eyes. 'And I love you for it.'

And then nothing was said for a long time.

My Inga, my wonderful, beautiful, smart Inga. Finding all that out.

And even more than that. Going to the council and getting them to officially call it Jacob's Street. Because even if he did do wrong, and we ain't – no, sorry, aren't – condoning that, at least we can recognise that he tried to make amends. Nobody's a hundred per cent bad any more than they're a hundred per cent good. Nothing can bring back the person he killed of course, but our combined rents still pour into that charity month after month, and only Inga and me know the real story behind it. We've sort of become the guardians of the street these days, especially now that we're getting married soon. Our main job, which is very easy, is to make sure that nobody falls behind in the rent.

Politeness Costs Nothing

The scene is the cabin of a small pleasure boat four miles off the coast of Canada. A man is sitting with his head in his hands. Presently he rises, gets pen and paper, and starts to write.

I am terrified. I don't like the water at all and I had hoped that I would never die by drowning.

Don't let anyone tell you that drowning is a peaceful death. It's a myth. Think about it for a moment. You can only hold your breath for so long. Then you're breathing in water. Which means there's no oxygen getting to the brain. And slowly, slowly your brain closes down, which means your heart stops beating. But it's not peaceful and it's not fast. It will be like being strangled slowly, kicking and squirming and jerking in agony. Which is why I'm terrified.

I can hear the two of them up on deck, preparing things, but they haven't tied me up because they know I can't escape. We're nowhere near land and I couldn't swim that far to save my life – literally! – even if I managed to break out of the cabin. So I'm writing this before it happens.

This waiting is the hardest part. If I thought they'd just dump me over the side and I'd go down like a rock, well, that would be better in its way. But I know what they'll do because I've done it with them, when I was one of them. We did it to Joe Glazman and Varlo Minetti and I personally did it to Fink Finkelstein, and Don Ramsay actually congratulated me on that job.

That was before I turned on him of course. Before I turned state's evidence, which changed everything. It put Don Ramsay inside for eight years, yes, but as soon as he got out, he and his men got me. I was a fool to think they'd never find me in that quiet village.

They tie you to a chair, see, and they put your feet in these tubs of quick-drying cement. And while it's drying, they're all politeness and gentleness to you. They'll ask me if I've got any last wishes. Well, my last wish would be to be shot in the back of the head, quick and painless; but then they'll only laugh and say, 'Sorry, bud, we're afraid we can't do that. It would make such a noise. It's going to have to be the traditional way.'

And they'll offer me a cigarette, but even if I was to accept, they'd laugh again and say, 'No, cigarettes are bad for you. You can die from smoking them.' And they'll laugh uproariously.

And how do I know all this? Because I invented a lot of it myself when I did the Finkelstein job, and that's why Don Ramsay liked it.

And when they take you out, tied to the chair of course and with your feet in the tubs of cement which has dried by now, they'll still be all apologies and politeness. I invented that too.

'Pity it's so cold,' they'll say, 'but they do say that hell is a lot warmer, and that's where you're going.'

Then the worst part.

I'm terrified of the water and they know it. So they'll work another of my inventions. Instead of just tipping me over, they'll lower me down on two ropes, slowly, so that the water laps over my ankles, then my calves, then my knees; I'll wince as the cold water hits my genitals, then it'll be up to my waist, then my chest. At that stage, usually, they pull you up a bit and let you dangle there before they start to lower you again. The water would get up to my neck and slowly, slowly they'll let the rope out an inch at a time until it comes up to my eyes. I'll be able to lift my head so that I can breathe precious air for a few more minutes – yes, minutes! – and then they'll lift me up a bit so's I can breathe normally, and all the time they'll be so polite and humble.

'Just wanted you to know what it's going to be like. Wouldn't want it to come as a surprise, you see.'

They'll do that a few times, pulling you up every time, and you don't know which is going to be the last time, and all the while they'll be so courteous and saying, 'Terribly sorry to have to do this to such a nice man, but you know how it is. Don Ramsay ordered us and we're not going against his wishes – not like some people.'

And when they finally leave me under long enough for all my bubbles to come up, their fun will be over and I'll be squirming in the chair and then they'll let me go and my agony will start, breathing water and my brain slowly atrophying and my heart slowly stopping. And then it will be over for me.

Not long to go now. I hate the prospect of being drowned slowly.

I am terrified.

Not long after he had finished writing, there came the sound of two men descending to the cabin. The door opened.

'Are you coming quietly, Walshie, or have we got to thrash you?'

Walshie smiled, a forced smile. 'No point in me resisting, Zac. It's going to happen anyway.'

'Come on then.'

But even so, the men held him, one on each side, as they walked to the tubs of wet cement.

'You want a last smoke?'

'No thanks, Zac. It'll only get damp as I go down. You can have it. Enjoy it.'

'Any last wishes?'

Walshie gave a strained laugh. 'No chance of a bullet in the back of the head, eh?'

This time the other man spoke. 'Don't be stupid. You know what's goin' to happen.'

'Ah yes, Jerksy, you always were quick to the point.'

'Put your arms behind your back, then,' said Zac. 'It's time to tie you in.'

'It's a good chair, this is, you know. You made it, didn't you, Zac? You should have been a carpenter.'

Walshie was able to hold his nerve to the end, but not without difficulty. As he was lowered over the side he glanced up and said, 'Aren't the stars beautiful?' And although it was quite some minutes before he died, they were the last words he spoke.

Back in the cabin, the two men sat at the table, drinking whiskey.

'Well, we done it,' said Jerksy. 'We done him in just like the Don ordered. But he didn't give us no fun, he was too polite. He was even more polite than we was.'

'He was frightened all right, though, wasn't he! Shit-scared, you could see. You can't hide that.'

'Yeah. I've seen 'em slobber an' beg an' scream, but this bastard threw it back at us.'

'Well, he invented it, after all. I was with him on the Finkelstein job. That was fun, him being so fucking polite and apologetic about everything.'

'Polite and what?'

'Apologetic. It means saying you're sorry.'

'Walshie was never sorry to see Finkelstein go. Why did he say he was sorry?'

'He wasn't really sorry. He was just being sarcastic, making out that Fink was really a good guy and everything.'

'I had to laugh when he told you what a good job the chair was an' you oughta be a carpenter.'

'I do a good job on the chairs. Pity they always end up in the drink.'

'Yeah, well, you'd make about as good a fucking carpenter as I would make a preacher.'

'Bullshit! I'm a good carpenter. What are you laughing at!? You're no fucking good at anything!'

'I'm good at tipping people over the side.'

'And you're going to advertise in the newspapers, are you? Professional killer available for hire, good at throwing people out of boats. Apply Jerksy fucking Stevenson, no fixed address.'

'No need to be sarcastic about it, you bastard. You're no fucking better. You do what the Don orders, just like me.'

'Well, I'm a good carpenter. Walshie said so.'

'Oh, that's all right then. I can see the advert now. Zac Turner, professional carpenter, good at building chairs for people to drown in.'

'I'll thump you, you fucking bastard.'

'Who's a bastard?'

'You are, and a bloody good one too.'

'Oh, fucking shut up and sit down.'

'I'm getting out of all this. I'm gonna set up and be a proper carpenter. I'm gonna go straight.'

'The Don won't let you.'

'I'll fix him. Then I'm going somewhere where they won't find me.'

'Oh yeah? Where?'

'Australia.'

'Aus-fucking-tralia? Where's that?'

'Other side of the world.'

'You don't know the language.'

'That just shows how ignorant you are. They speak English in Australia.'

'Don't call me ignorant!'

'You're as ignorant as a fucking slug. You don't know how to do anything except tip people over the sides of boats.'

'You can insult me as much as you like. I'm gonna tell the Don when we get back.'

But if anybody had been within earshot, which they weren't, they would have heard a sharp report and then a loud splash. Then they would have heard the sound of the motor starting up and would have seen the boat head back towards land. If they had had very good hearing, they would have heard the man saying to himself, 'Jerksy's no loss to anybody. He was a first-class prick.' And as he neared shore, he repeated to himself, 'Fix the Don. Get to Australia. Become a carpenter. Go straight. Change my name – that's okay. Thanks, Walshie.'

*

Report in major city newspapers a few days later.

Notorious gangster Daniel 'Don' Ramsay was found dead yesterday in his city apartment, shot through the head in what police believe was a gangland killing. Police are appealing for anyone to come forward with information that might help.

*

Conversation in the city police station.

'That Don Ramsay was a bad man. Thank Christ he's dead. Nobody's trying too hard to find his killer, not even the gangsters. Everybody was scared of him. They're all glad he's gone. Whoever it was has done us a favour. The man was scum.'

*

Small paragraph in the missing persons column of the August *Police Bulletin.*

Missing: Jeremy Stevenson, aka 'Jerksy' Stevenson. Of no fixed address. Mr Stevenson had a police record and was a known small-time gangster. He has not been heard of since going on a fishing trip in early July. Fears are held for his safety. Anyone knowing his whereabouts should contact their local police station.

*

Short article in a provincial Australian newspaper some twelve months later.

Mr Zachariah Truman has made quite an impression since he came here almost a year ago. This township needed a good carpenter and Mr Truman has filled the vacancy with distinction. If you want chairs, a table, or any kind of woodwork, Mr Truman – Zac to his many friends – is the man for you. He is always polite and his customer service is impeccable. In his spare time, Zac is a keen astronomer: he is fond of saying, 'The stars are beautiful.' Zac is considering joining the local Rotary Club, and he will be a welcome addition. This town needs more good citizens like Zac Truman.

Taxi

Ninety-seven. Ninety-seven! That's how old my great-grandfather was before he told me what he'd done in the Second World War. He'd never ever spoken about it and I knew that a lot of ex-soldiers didn't talk about their time in battle. And I always thought that his missing ear and missing hand were a result of wartime injuries. So I was surprised when he told me that he got them in 1938, a year before the war started.

'I wasn't even in the army,' he said. 'I was never in the army.'

I stared at him, open-mouthed.

'I was a tough,' he said. 'A small-time gangster. Only trouble was, I thought I was a big-time gangster. Thought I was smart.' He laughed. 'I thought I was being smart when I spat at the leader of the rival gang.'

He looked at me and his eyes narrowed. He held up his right hand, the artificial one, and he touched the hole in his head where his right ear should have been. 'That's how I got these,' he said. 'It taught me real fast that it's not a good idea to spit at your enemy when you're his captive. Not in the London underworld. Or anywhere else for that matter.'

He leaned back and took a gulp of lemonade. I've never known him to drink anything stronger.

'Well, it got me out of being shot at in the war,' he said with a sigh. 'Hell of a price to pay, though.'

'But I always thought you were a wartime hero,' I said.

He snorted. 'I was a taxi driver,' he said. 'A bloody taxi driver! In the war. In London.'

'How could you drive with only one hand?'

'Oh, they were desperate in those days. They fixed me up with a special cab that I could operate. Those were desperate times, Becky. Desperate times. You've no idea.'

'Desperate times?' I prompted.

'You've heard of the blitz, haven't you? You would've heard about it in school and you've probably touched on it in that university of yours.'

I nodded. 'I've seen a few films too,' I said.

'Hmph! I bet they glamorised the whole thing,' he said.

He leaned forward and his eyes narrowed. 'The people in London in the blitz were in just as much danger of being killed as a soldier at the front. Don't let anyone tell you any different. And they were innocent citizens! The Germans were coming over every night and bombing London indiscriminately. Every night for eight bloody months! The air raid sirens would come on and everyone would go into the air raid shelters. But their houses got flattened. Whole streets! And not everyone made it to the shelters. Old people especially found it hard. That's where your London taxi driver came in.'

I waited. His chin had grown firm and his top lip was stiff.

'The people today have got no bloody idea,' he said, almost to himself He turned to me. 'Look at this house we're living in,' he said. 'Imagine spending a sleepless night in a shelter and then coming home and finding it flattened to the ground. And every other house in the street too. Rubble and rubbish everywhere. But it's important that you get to another part of the city soon. You've got a job to do. There's a war on, remember. How do you do it, if the regular bus or train service has been put out? You call a cab of course. And the cab driver has to know how to negotiate around the rubble to get you where you want to go. And don't forget, not everything falls at once. Even the vibration of a vehicle can make a flimsy wall collapse. It's a wonder I survived!'

He sat back and took another drink while I tried to picture the scenes.

'Did I ever tell you about the woman who left her passport in the cab?' he asked.

Of course he'd never told us!

'She was Dutch,' he said. 'She'd fled to England when the Germans invaded. And she said she was going to America. Well, she'd be in a heap of trouble if she didn't have her passport with her! When I found it in the cab, I went to the immigration office and asked about her. They said just to hand it in and they would get it to her. I refused. Listen, Becky, being in a war makes you very suspicious. I wanted to make sure myself she got it. Fortunately, she'd mentioned where she was due to leave from. I went there and found her, gave the passport to her. Well, she was grateful, as you can imagine!'

He paused again and a twinkle came to his eye. 'She was very grateful,' he repeated, and let those words hang in the air. 'She still had a few hours before her ship sailed.' Then he grinned. 'Did I ever tell you you've got a half-Dutch great-aunt in America?'

No, of course he hadn't! 'But – but –' I stammered, 'Who is she?'

He gave a short laugh. 'Dunno. The woman wrote to me to say she'd had my daughter and that's all I ever heard. I don't know any more.'

'This is unbelievable,' I gasped. 'Are you sure you're not making this up?'

He grew serious. 'No, I'm not, Becky. You know me, I'm a bit of a rogue, but I'm not lying to you now. I'm ninety-seven, m'dear. I'm telling you straight.'

'Did you ever take any politicians anywhere?'

'Only a couple of times. Most of the time they had their own chauffeurs. But even chauffeurs can get killed in an air raid and then your regular taxi driver gets called in.'

'Who were they?'

'The politicians? Nobody really important. One was a fat greasy bastard who we all thought was enjoying the war. Who knows what he was up to behind everybody's back. The other one was a thin pale-faced fellow, looking worried sick all the time.'

'Who was he?'

'Don't know. As I said, neither of them were big shots. But it's funny, the fat fellow just paid his fare and got out. The pale man tried to give me a tip.'

'Tried?'

'It was a code of honour amongst us that we never accepted a tip during those times. Our little contribution to the war effort, if you like.'

He was quiet for a while, and so was I. I was beginning to regard this mischievous great-grandfather of mine in a new light.

He had always been one to speak his mind. He wasn't a grumpy old man, the sort who always insisted that life was great thirty years ago. Oh no, he was always looking forward in life. Even in his nineties, he never indulged in nostalgia. Which made it all the more surprising that he was telling me all this now.

Little did I know then what he knew. That he was dying from cancer. And I guess that he wanted some of his memories preserved. But when I mentioned the idea of a memoir to him, he thumped the table.

'No!' Even at ninety-seven he could still get angry. 'No! I'm not telling you this to make myself look important!'

'But –'

'I'm telling you this,' he said with tight lips, 'to make you realise that all of the heroism in the war wasn't all at the front. Those taxi drivers – me included – were every bit as brave in our own way as the soldiers. More so, in some ways. We were being bombed and we had nothing to fight back with – not personally. We had to depend on the skill of the anti-aircraft people and the fighter pilots.'

'And they did a great job from what I understand.'

'Yes, they did, but we still got bombed. And not only did we have to survive the bombings, we had to know which streets had been hit and where we could get from one place to another.'

'Did you ever come across injured people?'

I was surprised when his eyes twinkled.

'Yes, we all did. We all had to take a course in basic first aid.' His eyes twinkled again. 'How do you think I met your great-grandmother?'

'Was she a nurse?'

'No. She was a typist working in some government department. But I was taking her to work one morning when a wall collapsed and hit the side of my cab. It broke her leg and her arm. If I'd been a foot closer, it would've killed us both. That's how I got to know her. I tell you, Becky, you've got no idea how dangerous it was in those days.'

I tried to get him to talk more about the Dutch woman who had gone to America, but he was starting to clam up.

I leaned back and the peaceful Australian sun warmed my face. Then he was speaking again.

'At least my genes have spread around the world,' he said with a chuckle.

This was more like the roguish man I knew.

'There's us here in Australia. Your brother looks as though he's going to settle in England. Your mother's sister is happy in New Zealand. And there's my descendants, however many there are, in America.' He chuckled again.

Then he got up and went inside the house. 'Time for another lemonade,' said this man who had been a small-time gangster, a London cab driver in the blitz, and lived noisily and energetically after emigrating to Australia after the war.

I followed him into the house. 'Do you think we learnt anything from that war?' I asked.

He threw his head back and laughed, but it was a humourless laugh. But he said nothing, and that silence was as loud as a bomb.

Three weeks later, he was dead.

All the relatives came to his funeral, of course. And his mates too, no more refined or respectable than he was.

But, as one of the organisers of the funeral, I realised that something was missing. I phoned the local taxi company and asked if they could send someone to represent the taxi industry for his final farewell.

The taxi came and the driver stood respectfully at the graveside. He was an olive-skinned, middle-eastern-looking man.

After most people had gone, I spoke to him. 'Thank you for coming,' I said.

'Who was he?' he asked.

'He was my great-grandfather. He drove taxis in London in the war.'

At mention of the word 'war', my companion shuddered. 'I come from Afghanistan,' he said. 'It is very warlike there. And I am lucky to be here with my wife and child.'

As we talked, he told me of shattered villages, innocent civilians killed, maimed bodies and people running madly for shelter. The scenes he described sounded distressingly familiar.

'I am happy and safe here now,' he said. 'And I wish I could do more to honour your great-grandfather.'

'You can,' I said. 'To honour his memory, would you promise not to accept any tips for the rest of this week?'

'Certainly,' he said. 'Certainly. But why?'

'He never accepted any tips during his time as a taxi driver in the war.'

'That was his contribution, was it?' said the man.

'He contributed more than that,' I replied. 'Much more.'

He nodded in understanding, this refugee from that unhappy war-torn country.

Then I hugged him. 'Thank you for coming,' I said again. 'Thank you for coming.'

And as he walked away, I pondered again on the question about us ever learning anything from war.

The Man Smiled

He was a newcomer to town, only been there three weeks and didn't know anybody apart from his associates at work. The man, whose name is not important, had always been quiet and reserved, and that was perhaps why he was still unmarried in his early thirties.

He shopped in the supermarket, and along the aisle he noticed a woman who looked decidedly unhappy. At the checkout, the shoppers formed two queues and he found himself standing in line opposite the unhappy woman. She could be nice-looking, he thought, if only she could put a smile on her face. As they moved forward in their queues, he looked across at her and she suddenly looked across at him. He felt embarrassed but on an impulse he smiled at her.

And that has made all the difference.

Gregory Byatt was never so angry as when his wife left him. He ranted and shouted at her and almost hit her, a thing he had never done before. He was a red-faced angry man, quick-tempered at the best of times. His fault-finding had made his wife Eleanor consistently unhappy so that she had almost forgotten how to smile.

When she told him she was going to live with another man, he smashed his cup, smashed a plate and told her to get out right now! He wanted nothing more to do with her.

'And what about Trevor?' he demanded.

'Don't try and make me feel guilty,' she retorted. 'He's fifteen. He'll survive. He's more like you than me anyway. You're two of a kind.'

'Get out! Get out!'

And out she went to live with her new love, whose name is not important.

Angry men often suffer from black moods and Greg Byatt was no exception. He oscillated from irrational anger to deep despair. His wife had left him! Sometimes he would go out into the yard and smash stones with the sledgehammer, gritting his teeth and swinging wildly. Other times, he would sit motionless just staring at the wall.

Fifteen-year-old Trevor did not suffer from the Black Dog. He was a feisty, energetic youth who had always been closer to his father. His mother's leaving did not make him angry or depressed. His father was taking little notice of him: he was either venting his rage in the backyard or sitting motionless and unseeing. Trevor felt free, undisciplined, and that is not a good thing for a teenager with attitude. He was the leader of a pack of three; typical teenagers who thought they were tough and were looking for an outlet to prove it.

They found it in Williams. Williams the wimp, they called him, flicking bits of paper at him in class and deliberately tripping him up in the football games. Then it got worse. They started chasing him home from school, and once – only once because he was a fast runner – they caught him, filled his shoes with mud and made him walk home in them, squelching in discomfort, while they held their ribs in laughter behind him. It could have been worse, and both Byatt and Williams knew it.

'Next time,' Byatt breathed at him in class, 'next time we'll show you what we do to wimps.'

But the next time didn't come. Peter Williams was a good runner and he was scared, and fright gave him wings. Byatt's gang didn't have the sophistication to lay elaborate traps for him, but Peter developed eyes in the back of his head just in case. He lived in perpetual fear of being caught alone by the gang.

Byatt rejoiced in the other boy's suffering. He laughed as he saw the fear in his eyes every time he muttered a threat. His two cronies backed him up.

Peter Williams made sure he was out and running every day when school finished, and he stayed inside at the weekends.

His schoolwork suffered. Previously he had been a good student, possible university material, but now it started to go downhill. He became tense and timid, jumping at every sudden noise or movement. He developed black rings under his eyes. His mother noticed and thought that it was just juvenile hormones. Perhaps too much masturbation, she thought; he'll get over it. But she was not a suspicious woman and because Peter never confided in her, she saw no reason to worry. She had enough on her plate anyway. Peter's father had died a year previously and that had put a burden on both of them. Grief and unhappiness were constant companions in the Williams household.

There was one occasion when Trevor Byatt and his henchmen did catch Williams. He was running away from them on the way home when he tripped and fell and they caught up to him. They weren't vicious enough to kick him but they rolled him in the mud, laughing uproariously, until he got up and sprinted away. Then they had no chance of catching him again. He arrived home filthy dirty but reckoned he had got off lightly.

They took to sitting behind him in class. He became afraid to answer questions because he knew they would prod him from behind, or flick rubber bands to the back of his neck, or kick his ankles under the desk.

This was getting serious. His father was dead, his mother was unaware of his problems, and as a typical adolescent he felt incapable of sharing his troubles with her. He thought he should be able to handle them himself. But he felt totally inadequate. He stopped himself from crying, because men 'don't do that'. But inside, in his soul, he was keening.

Suicide came into his mind, as it will to teenagers with problems. He hated the thought because he knew it would be the final victory for his tormentors, but at least it would end his suffering.

He ate little, showed no interest in television or the computer or books or anything, and spent long periods alone in his room, just lying on his bed staring at the ceiling.

And while Trevor Byatt was going his swaggering bullying way, two people he knew very well were going through torments of the soul. His father was still agonising over his wife's desertion; and his school victim was entertaining vague thoughts of suicide.

And Byatt was unaware of both of them. As a typical self-absorbed teenager, he took little or no notice of his father's problems and he certainly did not know of Williams's mental condition.

Mr Le Compte had struggled as a teacher when he first started, and even now, in his third year, he still felt uncertain about his chosen career. He liked talking to his students and he felt interested in their welfare, but his actual teaching style had been criticised for not being clinical enough, not cut and dried and handed to the students on a plate, like the other teachers.

He made an effort to relate to the individual boys and girls in his classes, and as a result he was liked and respected by the students, even if his fellow teachers thought he was too soft on them.

'Adolescent kids have a lot on their plate,' he would say, remembering his own turmoils of those horrific times. 'I think they do well to remember anything at all we tell them in class. They need sympathy and understanding. Then perhaps they'll listen to us.'

The other teachers, hardened in the ways of the classroom, laughed at his perceived innocence. 'You'll learn,' they said. 'You'll learn.'

But in three years, his attitude had not changed. He felt an empathy towards his charges that came naturally to him and made him feel fulfilled.

The boy Williams, for example, seemed to be going through a rough period. He had been a good student, one of the best, but recently his work had been poor and his performance in the classroom had been weak.

Something is wrong with that boy, he thought, and he made a point of trying to find out what it was. He soon saw the problem. Byatt and his mates were bullying him. There was no mistake about it. Mr

Le Compte had often smiled at how much the teacher could really see from the front of the class. Contrary to what the students thought, the teacher usually knew all that was going on surreptitiously between the students. But if the teacher was to address each misdemeanour, there would be punishments and discipline all the time, and nothing would get taught.

Action is needed here, he thought. This is unacceptable. And Byatt is not stupid. He is worth talking to. His two cronies were weaklings who would soon find another source of amusement if he could get the bullying to stop.

'It's only a bit of harmless fun, sir,' said Trevor Byatt as he sat in Mr Le Compte's office.

'It may be harmless to you, Trevor,' said Mr Le Compte, 'But do you know what it's doing to Williams?'

'How do you mean?'

'It's destroying him. His schoolwork has gone downhill. Can't you see he's frightened of everything? He's scared of his own shadow. And that may be funny to you, but it's deadly serious to him. He's not a bad kid. And neither are you. Williams is a good runner, in fact. I've seen that.'

'Yes, I know he is, sir.'

'I want you to do something. Will you pick him to play in your next football game? Probably on the wing, where he can use his speed. You're usually the captain in your games and you get to choose your team. I'm asking you to do that, as a favour for me if nothing else.'

'All right, sir.'

Trevor Byatt thought he had got off lightly; he had been expecting a rocket from the teacher when he had been ordered into his office.

Came the next impromptu rugby football game where Byatt and Wesley, the two best footballers of the grade, stood and picked their players one by one. After the first few predictable choices had been made, Trevor Byatt astounded his mates by picking Peter Williams. Williams was usually one of the last to be picked.

'I think he might be good on the wing,' Byatt explained. 'He's a good runner.'

They lined up and the game started. Peter Williams knew what was expected. Get the ball and run like hell until tackled: or preferably pass the ball before being tackled. Simple.

Except that it didn't work out that way. During the whole game, he only got the ball once, and then he was immediately tackled and dispossessed before he could run. Trevor Byatt may have tried to give him a chance, but he had not counted on the other players ignoring him, thinking he was useless.

'What did you pick him for?'

'Okay, okay, it was a mistake. Williams is no good, we know that.'

Mr Le Compte was furious. Trevor Byatt was back in his office straight away.

'What was all that about, Byatt?' he demanded.

'I can't control the whole team, sir. I picked him like you said. If nobody passed the ball to him, it's not my fault.'

'Yes, it is! You're supposed to be the captain! A captain is more than just someone who picks the team and goes up to toss the coin. You're supposed to direct them. No wonder you lost. You've got to show some leadership. The next time you play, you must direct your team, give them a strategy, read the game and change tactics if you need to. And give the boy a chance.'

'You mean you want me to pick him again, sir?'

Mr Le Compte leaned forward. 'Byatt, I'm a teacher and you're a student. Believe me, I can make life very hard for you, within the rules, if you try to be smart with me. Now get out there, think about the qualities of leadership, and if I see you or your friends even think about picking on Williams, I'll come down on you – personally – like a ton of bricks. Now get out!'

Peter Williams found to his surprise that neither Trevor Byatt nor his mates chased him home that afternoon. He had expected a revenge because of his bad game, even though he knew it hadn't been his fault.

Two days later, they lined up for another game. Byatt picked Williams again, to gasps of disbelief from the others.

'Are you crazy? He's hopeless!'

'Listen,' he said. 'Gather round. Now, Williams here is a good runner. He's on the wing. Get the ball to him and try to keep up with him so he can pass it. And Williams, you know what to do. Run your hardest. Dodge if you can. Pass it if you can. And score a try if you can. Right, guys, Williams might just be our secret weapon, because the others will put their weakest player against him. Let's use our brains a bit. And back each other up.'

It would be nice to report that Peter Williams played the game of his life and scored the winning try or something like that, but it didn't happen that way.

They got the ball to him and he used his speed to gain valuable ground. Gaining confidence, he feinted a couple of times and managed to pass the ball to a team mate who scored a try.

And the opposition didn't get smart. They got nasty. When next he got the ball, they gave him no room to move. Three players piled on him and when they got up he stayed down.

'What's wrong, mate?' said Byatt the captain.

'My leg's killing me. I think it might be broken.'

'Sir!' shouted Byatt. 'Mr Le Compte! Williams here is injured. He thinks he's broken his leg.'

And so for the rest of the game the team played one man short while Peter Williams was taken to hospital and his leg put in a cast.

'What do you do now, Trevor?' said Mr Le Compte as they sat in his office.

'How do you mean, sir?'

'You were the captain of his team. He's injured. What does a good general do?'

'You want me to visit him, sir?'

Mr Le Compte smiled. 'Let's both go.'

Trevor Byatt managed to persuade his father to drive him to the hospital that evening. It was the first time Gregory Byatt had been out since his wife had left him, apart from going to work. Mr Le Compte was there already and shook hands with him in the car park.

'We won't be too long.'

'I'll wait for you in the car,' said the father.

Williams's mother was there with Peter when Mr Le Compte and Trevor Byatt came up to his bed. After introductions all round, the usual platitudes were spoken, little gifts given, expressions of 'Get well soon,' and 'You'll be back in the team in no time,' were spoken, and the two males left.

'That was nice of them to come,' said his mother.

'Yes,' said Peter, who was beginning to feel better already.

The next day at school, Mr Le Compte called Trevor Byatt into his office again. He put forward a simple question. 'What happens next, Trevor?'

Byatt thought he knew but didn't want to appear too friendly, not all at once. He waited for a prompt from his teacher, but Mr Le Compte just sat there, waiting for his answer.

Finally Byatt spoke. 'Should I go and see him by myself, sir?'

Mr Le Compte grinned. 'Trevor, you're developing the qualities of a good leader.'

Again, it would be nice to report that Trevor Byatt and Peter Williams became fast friends, but this is real life and real life doesn't always happen that way. Sure, the bullying stopped, Williams became a regular winger in the team once he had recovered, and Byatt came to trust that he would always play a good game. Peter's academic work started to improve. He felt better and more settled and looked forward to perhaps going on to university. Trevor Byatt's life improved too. He was no academic but he continued to work on his leadership skills.

One evening he spoke to his father. 'Dad, it's time you accepted the hard fact that Mum is gone and isn't coming back.'

Byatt senior looked up in surprise at his son. Instead of seeing an adolescent, he saw a serious young man who was taking an interest in his father's welfare. He didn't know what to say.

'Oh yeah?' he blurted. 'So what?'

'You need to get out, meet some other people. You're brooding too much.'

'Oh, listen to the wise counsellor,' sneered the father.

Trevor ignored the dig. 'How did you and Mum meet?'

'We met at a dance. I was a good dancer in those days. Could've gone into competitions.'

'Why don't you take it up again?'

'Nah! I'm too old. Who'd want to dance with an old man like me?'

'From what I've been told,' said his son, 'there's lots of mature women out there looking for a good man.'

'Well, that rules me out then,' laughed his father, and Trevor smiled too.

It was the first time he had seen his father laugh since his wife had left him. And he knew the seed had been sown. Time to let it germinate now without forcing it.

When the time came to leave school, he enlisted in the army, where he quickly rose through the lower ranks to become a sergeant. The men below him respected him because they knew that he was willing to work with them, to show them how to do things properly and to help them if they experienced difficulties.

After he left the army, he joined the police force and became one of the best cops on the beat. He wasn't interested in rising up the ranks of promotion; he figured that he could do more good by staying on the streets and helping the common man. Even the local criminals came to acknowledge that at least they would get an honest deal from this cop. Sure, he could be hard but he was always fair, and he knew when to temper justice with mercy.

Meanwhile, Peter Williams had graduated from university. Initially, he thought he might play for the varsity football team but soon discovered there were bigger, stronger and more brutal contenders there, so he abandoned those ideas and concentrated on his studies. He became a biologist. But his talents as a good runner did not go to waste; he joined the local athletic club and became a respected coach, eventually marrying one of his female charges and settling into a happy family life.

It is tempting to hope that Gregory Byatt, Trevor's father, found another woman and settled down, but real life is not always so neat. He joined the local dancing club and even entered a few competitions, but he didn't like the serious intensity of such events and settled for just enjoying himself twice a week. He dated a few women but nothing came of that; but at least he lifted himself out of his depression and started looking forward to life again.

The real change was to Mr Le Compte. After the Byatt–Williams affair, as he called it, he left the teaching profession and trained to become a counsellor. It was evident from the start that he had a natural talent for it. Through the years, he was responsible for the improvement of countless lives. He was one of those people whom everyone in town knows and likes. He not only helped the people in trouble, but showed them skilfully how they could help other people. It is no exaggeration to say that the whole spiritual and mental health of the town was very healthy and could be traced back to the influence of this one man.

So Mr Le Compte found his true calling.

Gregory Byatt put his past behind him and danced regularly.

Trevor Byatt was one of the best policemen the town has known.

Peter Williams became a happily married, confident young man.

Eleanor Byatt and her lover lived happily together.

And all because the man smiled.

The Vicar's Visit

'It's a right bloody mess! I go away on three weeks' holiday and come back to this. Weeds everywhere, vegetables going to seed, lawn ankle high. Couldn't you have done a little bit around the place?'

'Thomas! I will not have you speaking to me like that! You know it's the wrong thing to do. Now, you're the gardener, so get to work and bring it back to order.'

'Aye, well, it'll take a while. You can't recover from this inside a couple of days.'

'Well, I want you to concentrate on the front for a start. Mow the lawn at least. I want it to look nice because the vicar's coming to visit this morning.'

'Oh, the vicar! Yeah, you like him, don't you? And I reckon he fancies you too.'

'Now, Thomas, I'm getting tired of your crude innuendos. The vicar and I are good friends and he comforts me after his Lordship's death.'

Thomas went away, muttering. 'Aye, his Lordship wouldn't have let the garden get into this state while I was away. He didn't mind getting his hands dirty occasionally.'

Lady Marianne went into the manor house and up to her room, to prepare for the arrival of the vicar. As she sat at her make-up desk, she could see out of the window to where Thomas was working in the garden. She flushed slightly as she saw the vicar's car roll up and stop near Thomas. She watched as the vicar got out and spoke to him, but she was too far away to hear what they were saying.

The two men shook hands heartily. 'How're ye goin', you old bugger?' said the gardener.

The vicar beamed. 'I'm fine. And I can see that you haven't changed. You're still as crude as ever. You know you weren't brought up like that.'

'Yeah, well, you know and I know that it's all a show, ain't it? Between you an' me, the old girl likes me like that, you know.' And he gestured towards the manor house where Lady Marianne was nervously awaiting the vicar.

'It's just as well she does,' replied the vicar. 'Otherwise you'd have got the sack years ago.'

Thomas the gardener changed the subject. 'How's Mum?'

'She's fine. She sends her love as always. You really should visit her more often, you know.'

'Does she worry about you?'

'How do you mean?'

'Well, you not being married yet.'

The vicar gave an involuntary glance towards the manor house. 'I've got ambitions in that direction,' he said.

Thomas hadn't missed a thing. He chuckled quietly. 'Well you're not wasting any time. You've only been in the village six weeks and you've visited her at least once a week since you came here. And the old girl certainly ain't complaining,' he said.

'She's not so old. She's only a couple of years older than me.'

'You seriously thinking of asking her to marry you?'

The vicar smiled grimly. 'The thought had crossed my mind. But I've got a couple of worries.'

'What's them?'

'What do you think she'll say when she finds out that we're brothers?'

'Oh, I don't think she'll mind. She knows deep down that I'm not as rough as I make out, and I think she'll find out in time that you're not so much of a stuffed shirt as you first seem.'

'Well, coming from you I suppose that's a compliment,' grinned the vicar, and added, 'you old bugger.'

'Now, none of that,' laughed the gardener. 'I think she'll like you well-mannered.'

The two men walked around the garden.

'You've certainly got your work cut out bringing this back up to scratch,' said the vicar.

'Yep. I'll do it, no problem. But you said you'd got a couple of worries. What's the other one?'

'Well, it's a bit embarrassing. But she seems to me to be rather inhibited. I'm wondering what she'll be like in bed.'

Thomas threw his head back and roared with laughter. 'Don't you worry about that,' he said. 'I'm sure you'll find she's compatible. And think of the fun you'll have finding out!' He slapped his brother on the shoulder. 'Now get in there and give it your best shot,' he laughed.

The vicar smiled and strode inside and Thomas went back to his garden, sniggering to himself. He bent to the weeds but his shoulders still shook with laughter.

'Fancy him worrying about what the old girl's like in bed,' he chuckled. Then he looked up at the sky and, still grinning, thought, 'She's not bad. She's not bad at all.'

Transition

'Here's a likely one,' said the older man. 'We'll take him.'

'He's hardly old enough, is he?' said the other. 'He'd be no more than twenty.'

'Doesn't matter.'

'He looks strong enough too. Would we be able to handle him?'

'Of course we will. There's two of us. And we've got surprise on our side.'

'How will we do it?'

'You grab him from behind and hold him. I'll put a knife to him and demand everything he's got or we'll slit his throat.'

'What if he's got nothing?'

'Then we slit his throat anyway for wasting our time. Now quiet. Here he comes.'

The two robbers prepared to pounce but suddenly the younger one let out a scream.

'Aagh! I've been bitten! Aagh! A snake!'

The older man looked down in dismay. Their trap was blown. This young one was no good anyway. Time to get out of here!

The younger robber writhed on the ground in panic. 'I've been bitten! I've been bitten!'

The intended victim rushed up to him. He was a good-looking young man, barely out of his teens, but his face showed true compassion. 'Lie still! Lie still! Relax. Everything will be all right.'

With his strong hands, he held the man still and calmed him. He placed one hand on his forehead and the other on his heart. 'Relax,' he said. 'Have faith in me. Relax. The poison's going away already.'

The young robber lay still and gazed in amazement into the other's face. He felt calmer already. He sensed that there was nothing to worry about. He knew the snake had been deadly poisonous but now he felt untroubled by that. The man's hands on his head and heart had a calming influence and already he was starting to feel better. Strength seemed to flow from the man into his own body. He lay still and let it happen. His breathing became quieter and slower. He felt his thumping heart slow down. And he felt serene and calm and confident.

After a while, the man took has hands away and sat back.

The robber raised himself up and squatted beside him in the dust. 'What happened?' he asked.

'I'm not quite sure,' answered his saviour. 'I just felt as though I could help. I sort of felt a power that I knew I could use. It's never happened before.'

'Are you a physician?'

'No, I'm a carpenter. Or rather, an apprentice carpenter. I work for my father.'

'Where?'

'In Nazareth. I've been visiting some friends and I'm going back there now.'

There was silence for a little while and then the robber took a deep breath and said, 'I've never robbed anyone before. This was going to be my first job. The other fellow was going to show me how to do it but he ran away as soon as I got into trouble. The coward!'

'Perhaps you should forgive him,' said the Nazarene. 'For your own sake as much as his.'

'Yes, well, I don't think I'm cut out to be a robber. Would you mind if I came with you into Nazareth?'

'Not at all.'

They walked along side by side.

'With a talent like that,' said the ex-robber, 'you should become a professional healer.'

'I don't know,' said the young man. 'It was so strange. Almost as though some power was guiding me and I was able to channel the energy and healing into you.'

'Well, you want to work on it. You'll achieve a great deal if you can do that sort of thing all the time.'

The two men continued their walk under the hot afternoon sun.

'I think I'm going to stay in Nazareth and try to settle down there,' said the ex-robber. 'Get a job. And I'll keep in contact with you. You saved my life after all. If you can develop that talent of yours, I'll be your assistant: I'll follow you wherever you go. What's your name?'

'Jesus,' said the young man. 'And yours?'

'Judas. Judas Iscariot.'

Treating the Waiter

We've all heard it, of course. Probably from our mothers: 'If you want to see what your potential partner is really like, see how he treats the waiter.'

I was determined to remember that, this time. Because I needed to get myself a girlfriend. People were beginning to talk.

And I knew who I was going to ask.

She looked so lonely walking back to her table at the work canteen. She was fairly tall and slim and had short cropped hair which made her look slightly masculine. I like that in a woman. I was sitting with a couple of friends but I looked up at her and deliberately kept my gaze on her for longer than is conventional. She glanced at me and then looked away without any emotion. But that was okay. At least she'd seen me, and the next day I did the same again and this time she looked at me a little longer too.

Day three: time to move.

I made a point of sitting by myself at lunchtime and when I saw her sit down alone, I took my plate and went over to her. 'Hello,' I said, 'Can I sit with you?'

'Yes, if you want.'

Her whole demeanour, her look, her shyness, her insularity, told me instinctively that she was not used to men paying attention to her. I guessed that she'd probably never had a serious boyfriend, just like I'd never had a serious girlfriend.

'Where do you work?' I asked.

'In logistics.'

That was all. No elaboration, no reciprocating question. Hmm, this was going to be hard work. Take it easy, take it slow, I told myself.

I made a couple of comments about the weather, the awful canteen food, and the slowness of the works computers, and then I left it at that. We exchanged names – she was Elizabeth.

'Can I call you Liz?' I asked, and she didn't reply, which I took to be a 'no'.

'See you tomorrow,' I said as I left, and forced a smile.

At least she nodded and I was encouraged by that. I don't think she was a girl who was used to smiling a lot. Or to talking to young men, for that matter.

Take it slow, I kept telling myself. You really do need to get yourself a girlfriend if you're going to look respectable in public.

I made it a regular thing to sit with her at our lunchtimes. My mates poked each other and pointed and sniggered. In their minds, we were already an item.

Gradually, we got to know each other. She was a temporary employee – we call them temps – and her contract was due to finish in a week. So it was time to move.

'Could I take you out?' I asked. 'Perhaps we can go for a meal and then catch a film?' I knew she would hesitate. Perhaps she'd never been asked before.

But then she did say, 'Yes. Why not?'

We went to a decent little restaurant not far from the cinema. It wasn't going to be a high-flying, glamorous night. And I wasn't planning on coming on strong when it was time to say goodnight. Gradually does it, I thought. Just a nice meal, a good film, and a promise to meet again.

'Today was my last day at work,' she said.

We discussed her future work prospects over soup.

'I've got nothing coming up,' she said. 'I'm not sure what I'll do next.'

The waiter brought our main meal but as he approached he tripped slightly and a splash of gravy hit me on the shoulder.

'Oh sir, I'm terribly sorry!' he gasped.

It was then I remembered my mother's advice: 'If you want to see what your potential partner is really like, see how he treats the waiter.'

I forced a smile and said, 'That's okay. I can wipe it off. Don't worry about it.'

But the waiter still seemed aghast. He disappeared and came back with the manager of the restaurant. The manager apologised again and offered as compensation not to charge me for the meal.

I waved it aside. 'It was a small accident,' I insisted. 'Nobody's perfect. Forget it.'

The manager bowed his head in appreciation. He was a fit-looking, neat, compact man, clean-shaven with short dark hair. Both he and the waiter thanked me profusely and moved away.

I reckoned I had scored some brownie points with Elizabeth. She had seen how I had been magnanimous and I figured it had registered favourably with her. Perhaps soon she would allow me to call her Liz.

The rest of the evening went off as planned. We saw the film, I drove her home, and then wondered if I should steal a kiss as we said goodnight.

We had made another date to meet again in a couple of days so she just said, 'Thank you. See you Thursday,' and then she was gone.

This was slow work, I knew, but that was all right. I had a girlfriend and I was content with the way things were going.

We were going to meet at the same restaurant on the Thursday evening, and I got there with a few minutes to spare. A different man brought me a drink as I sat and waited, and then to my surprise the manager came out, stood beside me and put his hand on my shoulder.

'Come into my office,' he said.

What the hell's going on? I thought, but I followed him.

We sat down and he lit a pipe. I've always liked pipe smoke and it was nice to see him light up. He must have been only a few years older than me, well dressed, cultivated and good-looking.

'I have some news for you,' he said.

I waited.

'Simon – that's the waiter from the other night – and your girlfriend have run off together.'

'What?!'

'She came back the following night and they were together for a long time. Then he came and gave me his resignation. He told me that your girl had thought you were too mild on him and she had lost respect for you. And Simon told me that he had deliberately spilled that gravy to annoy you, because they had known each other before and when he saw her again, he got jealous and wanted to make you look bad in front of her.'

Well, so much for her never having had a boyfriend before, I thought.

'Instead, you went the other way,' he continued. 'You were too soft on him. Girls like a stronger approach, you know. If you must go with them, you've got to be a bit more assertive, my friend.'

I sat, dumbfounded. I obviously wasn't very good in my judgements of women.

'He's given me a forwarding address but I recommend you don't follow it up. What's the point? They're happy with each other and you have to admit you weren't getting very far.'

'No, I wasn't,' I admitted.

He really was a handsome guy, and that pipe suited him. It made him look somewhat sexy. His whole looks, manner and bearing spoke of charm and intellect. I was impressed.

'I'll miss him though,' he said. 'He was a good waiter. He had a knack of being able to size people up very quickly. He saw through you straight away.'

He paused.

'Let it go,' he said at length. 'Follow your natural instincts, my friend.' He looked at me and touched my arm. 'Who needs girls anyway?' he said, and his eyes twinkled as he sucked on his pipe.

Walk a Mile In My Shoes

This is not a nice story. If you're looking for something warm and fuzzy, go somewhere else. What's that old saying? 'Don't judge a man until you have walked a mile in his shoes.'

So listen to what I have to say.

There are two things you need to know about me. One, I am Jewish. And two, I was a young man in Germany in the 1930s and 40s. And if you know anything about history, you'll know what that means.

Being a German Jew in those days was hard; harder than you could ever imagine. But after Hitler came to power, my father could see what was going to happen and sent me to a quiet town in the country, to a distant cousin who was adept at forging documents. He later became very important to the Jewish escape movement in those turbulent times, but that is another story. He furnished me with the documents for a new identity, even including a certificate to say that I was disabled and couldn't fight in the war that we all knew would come. I was lucky, because I don't look Jewish.

I had to leave the town where I was born and raised because too many people knew me there for me to keep my secret very long. I moved to Berlin and with my new name got a job as a minor clerk. That suited me. I just wanted to keep my head down and survive this horror.

It was hard to keep in contact with my family. It would have been far too risky to send mail, but the Jewish underground movement provided me with the occasional opportunity to learn that my parents and two young cousins were still safe – for the moment.

You've probably read about all the persecutions that took place, but have you ever really stopped to think about it? I was there and although I wasn't targeted, being a bogus Gentile, I had to stand by helplessly while an innocent Jewish girl was raped in front of a jeering crowd of soldiers, then dragged off, no doubt to be the plaything of the officers until they grew tired of her and killed her. Such things were common in those days.

I couldn't protest because even one word of sympathy for 'the dirty Jews' would bring the Gestapo down on me, and too much investigation of my ancestry would be fatal. The only thing I could do was to keep quiet and hope it would end soon. But of course we all know that it didn't.

Then I heard how my mother had been raped and then shot, just like that. The man just walked away and left the helpless witnesses to clean up the mess.

I had a leaden feeling in my stomach every morning when I woke up, because I felt I was betraying my people; but the instinct for survival is very strong and I trudged through each day, doing my menial duties, offering no opinions and speaking to as few people as possible.

The personnel in the office where I worked were constantly changing as men were drafted into active service. Some, devout Nazis, were eager to go; others went reluctantly. I wondered how long it would be before the authorities took a harder look at my certificate of disablement and decided that I was fit enough anyway to go and be shot at.

Girls worked in our office too and although I tried to keep distant from them, male testosterone won in the end. Greta was a typical German, tall, blonde and healthy. Her desk was next to mine and it was inevitable that we would become friendly.

Her upbringing had been quite different from mine. She had grown up in the 30s never knowing real hunger, was an ardent admirer of Hitler, and a member of the Nazi party. I couldn't tell her that the reason Hitler was so revered in those early days was because he had robbed the Jews of all their wealth and distributed it amongst the poor, 'pure' Germans. No wonder they loved him!

I told her I had had a car accident and had suffered an injury to my spleen, which prevented me from active service. There is no greater lubricant to love than sympathy, and it took a better man than me to resist her words of comfort, her sweet kisses and her tender touches. I was twenty-six by then, she was two years younger, and we both thought we could see the possibility of a bright future together.

'Must we wait until we're married before...?' and she let the question trail off. But it was obvious what she meant. And although the next little while was gloriously beautiful, that was where my real troubles began.

I am Jewish, remember. And that means I am circumcised.

Greta said nothing after our lovemaking; in fact, she was unnaturally quiet. I thought I had failed to fulfil her, assured her that the first time is often the worst, and promised her, and myself, to be better at making love in the future.

But the future turned out quite differently.

We met the following day as planned, and that night we made love again. But she seemed distant.

When we had dressed and were sitting drinking coffee, she said, 'I want to talk to you.'

'Yes?'

She looked straight at me, pushed her face towards mine, and her eyes narrowed. 'You're Jewish, aren't you?'

'Of course I'm not!' I retorted swiftly – perhaps a little too swiftly. 'What makes you think that?'

She spoke quietly. 'You're circumcised.'

I knew I had my back to the wall. 'Plenty of Germans are circumcised.'

'No, they're not.'

'I – I had an infection when I was a child. I had to be circumcised.'

But she had noticed my stumble. 'You're Jewish,' she repeated, 'but don't worry. Your secret is safe with me...provided...'

'Provided what?' I asked, and then bit my lip. Just saying that was admitting the truth.

'Well,' she said – and now she was all business. 'How much is your life worth? We both know what will happen if you're found out.'

'Yes. So?'

'Half your wages every week.'

I gasped. This was blatant blackmail. 'I can't live on only half of what I'm earning!'

She smiled, and that smile was humourless. 'You're going to have to try.'

Now it was time for my eyes to narrow. 'And,' I said, 'what do you think they'll do to you if I tell them you've been sleeping with a Jew?'

'Oh, you'll never do that.'

'What makes you so sure?'

'Because that would be admitting that you're Jewish yourself.'

And that of course was true. This girl, who I had thought I was in love with, was proving to be as dispassionate and cold-blooded as any Nazi official.

Well, that love affair was over. They say that love and hate are two sides of the same coin and in this case it was true twice over. I had loved Greta but now I hated her. Or did I? She could have betrayed me but now she was saving my life, albeit at a great cost to me. So should I really hate her or should I be grateful to her? What a dilemma.

But then I thought about myself. Like anyone, I loved myself, that's only natural, but when I thought about it I began to despise myself. Here was I, working for the regime that was systematically murdering my people every day, and on top of that I was paying money to a Nazi party member just to save my miserable skin!

I knew I was being cowardly. I knew I was being a traitor to my people. But I wanted to live.

Then one day Greta was not at her desk. When she had not attended for a few days, I made casual enquiries, thinking she might have been sick, and was informed that she had volunteered to go to eastern Poland as a prison guard.

I didn't know whether to be glad or sad. Now I would not have to pay her my blood money. But as a good Nazi party member, perhaps she had betrayed me before leaving?

I didn't have to wait long to find out.

I was sitting at my desk when the personnel officer came and sat beside me. He had a pleasant smile on his face but I was immediately wary. 'Mr. Kruger,' he said, 'could we have a word in my office, please?'

In there, he invited me to sit down and said, 'We're just doing routine checks on everybody's background. That's all normal, as you know. But we seem to have found some anomalies in your details.' He looked me hard in the eye. 'Are you sure your name is Helmut Kruger?'

I quailed internally but this was no time to be shaky. 'Of course I am!' I said indignantly. 'What are you talking about!?'

'Do you have documentation of your ancestry?'

'Yes,' I said. 'Not with me, of course. I have it at home.'

'Please bring the documents in tomorrow.' His voice was cold and friendless now. He dismissed me and I walked in a daze back to my desk.

Of course I had lied. I had no documentation of my so-called Aryan ancestry. I had the forged documents about my own identity but nothing to show about my parents or grandparents. What was I to do?

It would be far too suspicious to report sick while I raced back to my distant cousin to get false documents about my ancestors. Once the Nazis' suspicions were aroused, it really was a case of being guilty until proved innocent. And it would be useless to say I couldn't find the papers. That would mean a search of my apartment, where they would be bound to find something to reveal my Jewishness.

I cursed Greta and my own weakness in getting involved with her.

There was only one thing for it: escape!

When I got home that evening, I immediately started bundling essential belongings together. I had heard that Sweden was a comparatively safe place to go. From there, I could make my way to England, or America. Anywhere away from this madness. I was even starting to look forward to it.

Then came the moment that really did change my life – just like countless other Jews.

A knock on the door.

My heart ran cold, but there was nothing for it.

When I opened it, there was a Gestapo agent.

'Samuel Braunstein?' he said.

Now when you have lived with one name for twenty-six years, it is very hard to conceal that fact. The man immediately noticed the twitch in my eye and even before I had time to deny it he had me by the scruff of the neck and was bundling me into a secured car.

That's when my nightmare began.

I had no option but to reveal my true identity, and with their typical efficiency they marked me on a list and put me on a train along with hundreds of other Jews, to a camp west of Berlin.

I am not going to describe detail by detail what happened over the next months – in fact, it lasted nearly three years. And every day felt like a lifetime, a hurdle, an ordeal to be got through. There has been enough documentation of such nightmarish happenings that I don't want to remember it. It was enough – it was more than enough – to have to go through it at the time.

The humiliations were the worst. In some strange way, we reasoned that there was a certain dignity in being killed. But to be constantly tormented, forever told that we were filthy subhuman pigs – that was worse in its way than being shot outright. Or gassed.

Of course we were filthy! We were made to work in even the worst of weather, latrine conditions were primitive at best, and we had no washing facilities. Of course we were filthy! How could we be otherwise?

I want to stop thinking about it but I must go on to tell you my story.

Because I was a young strong man, I was not killed as so many of my companions were. I was put to work. First it was building more huts to accommodate more and more Jews as they came in. Then they moved me into a factory making armaments. I proved to be not so good at that and as I weakened I was given the job of collating the lists of people being transported to other camps. We all knew what that meant: almost certain death in the gas chambers.

One winter's morning, a guard came up to me and said, 'Clean my boots.'

That was not uncommon. Why should they do their own cleaning when they had slaves who would do it in fear of their lives?

I knelt down and cleaned his boots, making sure they were absolutely spotless before I finished. I had seen prisoners shot for leaving the tiniest speck on a guard's boot when ordered to clean them.

As I knelt there with him standing over me, I couldn't help thinking that I would like to walk a mile in those boots. Just to feel a full belly and the comfort of a fire and perhaps even a warm bed: simple things that were denied us in our huts.

When I had finished, I was surprised to see him smile.

'What is your name?' he said.

'Samuel Braunstein, sir.'

And at that moment I thought the end had come. It was often their way to ask your name with all politeness and then nonchalantly take out their gun and shoot you for some imaginary fault. It was a favourite game of theirs.

'You have done a good job, Braunstein,' he said. 'Well done.' And with that he strode away.

I breathed again. Perhaps death would not visit me today.

A few days later, I had occasion to be involved with him again.

One of my smaller jobs was to count how many people had died in the night and report the number to the camp commandant. That was not as easy as it sounds. Sometimes, between my count and my report, more Jews would die. And when they came to drag the bodies out to the pit, they would see that my figures were incorrect. The commandant didn't understand; or rather, he didn't want to understand. It was just another opportunity for him to beat a helpless Jew for getting things wrong.

I'd worried about Asher for a long time. Every morning, I'd expected to find him dead. But he clung tenaciously to life. Why, I don't know. Surely death was better than this hell on earth.

There was the smell of death all around.

The guard whose boots I had cleaned noticed my concern over Asher. 'He won't last much longer,' he said, and I nodded in agreement.

On this particular morning, it should have been our Sabbath day but of course we had no opportunity to celebrate that. It was business as usual in hell.

It was pouring rain but that made no difference to what I had to do. Soaked to the skin, I went my miserable rounds of all the huts, tallying up the ones who had died in the night. Then it was my job to take the figure to the commandant and hope that no one suddenly died in the meantime.

Asher was still clinging to his fragile hold on life.

I was just about to climb the steps to the commandant's office when the same guard came up to me.

'Braunstein!'

'Yes, sir?'

'Asher has just died,' he said. 'You must adjust your figures to avoid another beating. He was a brave man.'

I looked at him in surprise. 'Why have you told me this? Why have you taken pity on me?'

He looked around to make sure no one else could hear. 'You don't think I really approve of all this, do you?' he asked, waving his arms to encompass the whole miserable camp. 'If I have the opportunity to help someone, even in the smallest way, I want to take it now. I've seen so much death. I want to have at least a couple of good marks against my name on judgement day.'

'If you're so concerned about what will happen to you on judgement day, why did you take this job in the first place?'

That was really taking a risk on my part, speaking to him like that. Many of the guards would have taken that as an excuse to beat me. But continual exhaustion and hunger had made life less precious to me than before. Like many Jews in the camp, I felt that I would welcome death for the peace it would bring.

'I was just too old – by a few months – to be called into the regular forces,' he said. 'And I was also unemployed and hungry. I needed a job. But they didn't tell me it would be like this.'

'And you can't leave now, of course,' I said.

'No. I must do my duty. Now get in there and take the opportunity to get your figures right for the day.'

I cannot say in truth that the two of us became friends after that. Under the circumstances, that was impossible. He was a capable and competent guard.

But it did seem he gave me a certain amount of protection – at least as much as he could. He had to be very careful, of course. If he was seen by any of his colleagues favouring the Jewish 'scum', he would have been punished most severely: possibly even executed. But he did manage to secretly slip me a morsel of food occasionally, and I have to say that I probably owe my life to him, because when we were liberated I was still alive.

I will never forget that last day when the Allies finally arrived. We had been hearing battle sounds all day and it was obvious that they were getting closer. That was a very dangerous time. Some of the guards shot themselves rather than be taken prisoner and tried as war criminals. Some of them shot the remaining Jews – those they could find. And some of them escaped.

Franz Muller – that was 'my' guard – was one of the ones who succeeded in escaping. But before he disappeared, he did one last thing for me. With shots ringing out as guards fired indiscriminately, he came to my hut where I was lying terrified. 'Come!' he barked, and grabbed my arm before I could react.

Now, a Jew weakened by nearly three years in a concentration camp is no match for a well-fed German guard. I thought I was going to be lined up and shot. It was complete chaos, complete anarchy.

But he pushed me into a quiet storage building and opened a cupboard door. 'In here!' He shoved me in and closed the door.

And that was the last I saw of him for over ten years.

I stayed in that cupboard for two days. I could still hear the shots, but they grew less frequent and then stopped altogether. All the killing had been done. For hours, there was silence but I still stayed there. But finally hunger and thirst drew me out: and what a sight! Bodies everywhere! I was used to death but this was different. Many of the bodies were of guards who had committed suicide rather than be taken prisoner.

But more than that was the sight of American soldiers! Liberation had at last arrived! Of course it was too late for so many of my people, and I wept beyond control. But I was alive! I had survived! And the Americans gave me food! Food! Food that I had been denied all those years. And I wept again.

They put me into a hospital and gradually, gradually I regained my strength. It took a long time. If you have been starved and abused continuously for three years, closely acquainted with death and never knowing when it is going to end, you do not recover in a few weeks. We were liberated in early spring but I lay recovering, then slowly walking, then slightly more vigorous, through the whole of that summer.

It was late autumn when the doctor came and spoke to me.

'You will be released in a few days' time,' he said. 'What will you do?'

I had thought about that. 'I'll return to my home town and see if any of my family are still alive. Although I doubt it. I know my mother's dead. But I'll search for my father and my two young cousins.'

But it was hopeless. I managed to get a job but my spare time was spent on trying to trace my family. Conditions at that time were chaotic. Many German towns were in ruins and mine was no exception. So many people had been killed towards the end and no one had had any time to document them. The only thing anyone could do was hope they wouldn't be killed themselves. When I told the people at the displaced persons centre that I was trying to trace my Jewish relatives, they either laughed or looked terribly guilty, but their answers were always the same.

'You're wasting your time, young man. All the Jews were taken away from this town. None have survived.'

There was only one other Jewish person searching for missing family. A nice-looking, dark-haired girl named Rebekah. We both agreed it was a forlorn hope.

'What happened to you in the war?' I asked. 'Where were you sent?'

She mentioned a concentration camp in Poland and I struggled to remember that name. I knew I had heard it before. Then suddenly it came to me. That was where Greta had been sent.

I mentioned Greta's name to Rebekah. 'Was she a guard at your camp?'

'There was a guard by that name, yes,' she said.

I couldn't resist my curiosity. 'What was she like? Was she sadistic or comparatively kind?'

'Neither really. She was just another guard. She did her job.'

'And what happened to them when the Russians came through?'

'The Russians! They didn't hesitate! They lined up all the guards and shot them. We all thought they were going to shoot us too, but they just told us to go.'

So Greta was dead. I felt a pang, I cannot deny it – and that pang haunts me still. Because it was not a pang of grief, but of – well, almost pleasure. Certainly of vindication. Greta had got her just reward, I felt. And then I immediately felt ashamed of thinking like that. But walk a mile in my shoes, reader: try being a Jew in a German concentration camp during the war because you have been betrayed by your former lover, and see if you do not feel some satisfaction when you learn that she did not survive.

But no, you can't try that of course, and I wouldn't wish that on anyone.

I told you this was not a nice story.

It was time for a new chapter in my life. I moved to Munich and got a job as a clerk. Then I sent for Rebekah and we got married under the canopy in the Jewish tradition.

For the first time in years, we were able to look forward to the future. And I knew what I wanted to do. It would take a lot of work but after what I had been through I knew now that I had the necessary endurance. But more than that, I wanted to help other Jews, fellow survivors of the holocaust, and I figured I had the intellectual ability to do it. I was going to train to be a rabbi. It was a late start for me. Most rabbis begin studies very early but I had not had that opportunity.

What followed was perhaps the happiest period of my life. The Jewish population in Munich was very small, as you may imagine, but Rebekah and I were part of a close-knit community and I received encouragement and support. I loved the lessons, the long hours of study, the prayers and the dedications. I felt that I had found my true destiny at last.

Towards the end of my training, I went to Paris to study for three months under a very highly regarded rabbi. I liked Paris and I enjoyed my lessons there.

But one day I was sitting at a pavement café when a man came and sat next to me and said, 'Hello, Samuel.'

I looked up and my eyes widened with amazement. Franz! Franz Muller, my old guard who had saved my life. Here he was in Paris. And more amazing than that – he was wearing the cassock of a Catholic priest!

I could only gasp, 'What are you doing here?'

He smiled. 'Well, as you see, I am now a priest.'

'But – but – how?'

He smiled again. 'It's a long story. Come to my apartment and we can share a drink.'

In his apartment, we sat comfortably as the light faded outside, and he told me his story.

'When the Americans came,' he started, 'I left that camp as quickly as I could.'

'After saving my life!' I interrupted.

He nodded and continued. 'The first thing I did was to get out of my uniform. I remember what we guards used to say to each other as the war drew to a close. "Enjoy the war because the peace will be savage." I went into the nearby town and had a stroke of luck. There were still plenty of bodies around, German soldiers who had died trying to defend the Fatherland against the Allies. I found a body and took the uniform, and also his identity documents, and then went in search of Americans to surrender to. That wasn't hard. They treated me coldly but they didn't beat me or kill me. I spent over a year in their prison but they had no interest in just another common foot soldier who had merely been following orders. They didn't know, of course, that I had been a concentration camp guard, or it would have been much worse for me. When I was released, I wanted to amend in some small way for the bad things I had done. So I decided to study to be a priest. But I have kept the identity of that dead soldier. Now I'm known by a different name. Now I'm Father Manfred Beck. I have only been qualified for less than a year and I'm working in a nearby parish. But I cannot disguise my German accent and, as you may imagine, many French people do not like me. So I'm happy that I'll be transferred back to Germany and I've just been told that I'll be working near Munich after next month.'

'Munich!' I said. 'That's where I am.'

'What are you doing there?'

'I'm married and I'm training to be a rabbi.'

He threw his head back and roared with laughter. 'From a guard and a prisoner to a priest and a rabbi!' he cried. 'Our lives have a certain parallel, my friend.'

'In more ways than one,' I said.

'How do you mean?'

Then it was my turn to tell him of my own change of identity, to try and avoid being imprisoned as a Jew, and of how I had been betrayed by my lover, and of my feeling of vindication after learning she had died.

He grew serious. 'As a Christian, it's my duty to tell you to forgive,' he said. 'And I know how terribly hard that will be for you, after what you have been through.'

'Maybe I can forgive her,' I said. 'And I can certainly forgive you. But can I forgive the whole German race for what they did to the Jews?'

He bent his head and a tear fell. He nodded, still looking at the ground. 'I understand,' he said. 'I understand.'

We parted then and we arranged to meet again when he was in Munich.

And he was the only Gentile who I invited to my graduation ceremony as a rabbi.

There are not many Jews left in Europe now, but Father Manfred Beck takes every opportunity he can to come to our small communities and try to reconcile the differences between Christians and Jews.

And I think about my life, and I know he thinks about his.

Did I do wrong to try and hide the fact that I am Jewish when so many of my people were being killed?

Was it wrong for me to feign disability so that I wouldn't have to be called into active service?

Was it wrong to feel a certain satisfaction when I learnt of Greta's death? That still haunts me, but his advice about forgiveness is a comfort.

And what of my friend?

I feel a certain power over him. I could betray him, even after all these years, and he would be tried as a war criminal. It would even the score for what Greta had done to me. But I have chosen not to. What good would it do? He is living a good life now, helping people, and it would be wrong to take that away. In that sense, I am perhaps protecting him as some sort of payment for the protection he gave me in the camp.

And I feel guilty, again, for feeling that smugness about myself. For knowing that I am 'doing the right thing' by not giving him away.

Did he do wrong to take the job as a guard instead of virtual starvation? Did he do wrong to change his identity to save himself after the war?

Or are those sins, if that's what you want to call them, appeased by the acts of goodness that he and I have done in our roles as religious leaders?

We sometimes talk about all this. What will the Supreme Judge say to us when our time comes? And we both agree: we cannot change the past, we can only try to make the future better for others.

All that matters is that we try to do good, try to help our fellow man at every opportunity. And we must leave it to the Supreme Judge to weigh the balance.

I have said that this is not a nice story. I'm sure that Father Manfred's past haunts him in his quiet moments. And I will never really be at peace with myself.

Walk a mile in our shoes, reader, and judge us if you must. But remember you are not the Supreme Judge.

You Rescue Me, I Rescue You

Laurie

> Labour and woe shall fill thy days, and memory
> Haunt all thy bitter paths.
>
> Rupert Brooke

They decided to go under the fire escape of the big grocery warehouse that night. They knew it was sheltered and it was unlikely they would be disturbed.

They squatted among the empty bottles and the blown-in old newspapers. Three bottles of wine were produced: one each. For a while no one spoke. The wind came in gusts and raised little whirls of grit and old paper. It would be a cold night.

'I wouldn't mind bein' in bed with a young bird right now,' said Tom, and Ted took the bottle from his lips to smirk in agreement.

'When I was your age, I could have,' said Laurie. 'Or nearly, anyway.' His hand trembled as he raised his bottle. The years of gutter living had marked him. His pockmarked face and rheumy eyes belied the fact that he was still only in his mid-forties: ten years the senior of his two companions.

'How come?'

'Well, I'll tell you,' said Laurie. His bottle was almost half empty already.

Tom and Ted settled back. It would help pass the time, they thought.

'I suppose it really started,' began Laurie, 'when my wife left me. She said I drank too much even then. But I wasn't bad. I didn't drink all that much. Anyway, she didn't like it. She said she'd leave me and I tried to pull myself together. Then I lost my job. Couldn't get another. Things were bad. Anyway, she left. What really hurt was that she never let me know where she went. That wouldn't've been so bad if it hadn't've been for little Julie. Four she was. With long ringlets down to her shoulders. Blonde. She was a lovely little girl. I haven't seen her since they went.' He took a long pull from his bottle.

'What about the bird?' said Ted.

'I'm coming to that, I'm coming to that. Anyway, after they left, I went bad. Gambling. Drinking. Fighting. Couldn't hold a job. Fell behind in the rent and got thrown out. By that time, I didn't care. I wasn't worried if I lived or died. Then the Salvation Army got me.'

'Oh Gawd!'

'Oh, they weren't too bad. I'd been sleeping in this park and they took me to their place and gave me a hot bath and a feed. They offered to help me get a job. I told them I didn't care. I'd got nothing to live for. But at least they kept me clean. I think I could've come good then if only I'd known where my little Julie was.'

He sighed. Another drink. A pause.

'Anyway, this girl starts coming in, see. She was in the Salvation Army and had just moved into the area. She tried to help me again. Shirley, her name was, and she sort of made it her business to look after me. And she did a damned good job too. She was a nice girl. I started washing and shaving because I knew she'd come to see how I was. Then I started cutting the drink down. Me and Shirley used to sit and talk. She said she'd come from the country and that her father had died. She'd come into the city to get a job. I think she was very lonely One day, she said there was a cleaner's job going where she worked if I'd like to give it a go. I hadn't worked then for nearly nine years. So I gave it a try and, well, it's surprising how different you feel when you've got a few dollars in your pocket. Then she got so's she'd stay behind when she finished work and help me with the cleaning. That way, we finished earlier and then we'd go for a meal. She said she liked talking to me. I tell you, she was a damn nice girl. I'd given up the drink altogether by then. We got so that we were going to church together on Sundays.'

'Bloody church?'

'Oh yeah. They're not a bad mob, y'know, the Sallies. Anyway, this young bloke at church used to talk to her a lot and I could see he fancied her. So I asked her one night what she thought of him. She said she liked him but she liked me better. Then she said she loved me. Just like that. Looked me in the face and said she loved me.'

'So what did you do?'

Laurie did not answer. He was staring into his bottle.

'What did you do, Laurie?'

Laurie stirred. 'Well, I tried to talk her out of it, didn't I? Said I was too old for her. But she wouldn't have it. So…well, so we started going together, sort of official, like.'

'Yeah,' said Ted with a snigger, 'I know what you mean.'

'Oh, nothing like that,' said Laurie. 'She was strict Salvation Army, remember. Anyway, I could see this young bloke still fancied her and that he was upset 'cos she was going with me. He seemed a decent sort too. Well, I'd been at the job for exactly six months, so I thought I'd celebrate. It was the longest job I'd had in years. I gave her the slip one night and went for a couple of drinks. But it got hold of me. I ended up spread across the footpath. When I sobered up, I knew it was all over. I'd tried my best, but…'

He sighed, a long quivering sigh. He took another pull at his bottle.

'I took some drink in with me to work that night and I was pretty sozzled even before the boss left. He called me into his office and I abused him. Tried to pick a fight. He called Shirley in 'cos he knew we were sort of together. She pleaded with him to let her sort it out but I caught him a clip behind the ear. That finished it. It was all over. I never saw her again. It's a lousy picture to carry of someone the last time you saw them: all huddled over and crying.' He looked at his bottle. It was almost empty.

The wind came in cold, sharp gusts. Dust blew around them.

'Ah, she'll be happy now,' he said. 'No risk. She'll be married with a couple of kids and a nice house and a good husband.'

Why was it, he thought, that people always thought that derelicts were brutes? In actual fact, he thought, derelicts were people who were too sensitive to take the blows of life. The brutes were the people who could cope.

His voice was thicker. 'Yeah, she'll be all right. She was a damn nice girl. I wonder where my little Julie is now.' His head sagged forward and his body settled slightly.

Ted looked at Tom and grinned. 'Ol' Laurie can spin 'em, can't he!' he said. 'Ol' Laurie can spin 'em.'

Tom laughed in agreement.

They looked up. Two women in uniform were walking towards them. 'Look out! Sallie's Army. Let's scarper!'

So the two bums slipped away round the corner, leaving their companion, whose chin had fallen on his chest, his tongue lolling out, a dribble of saliva running onto his coat and his cheeks slightly moist.

Laurie and Shirley I

Work is love made visible.

Kahlil Gibran

She was devastated when her father died. She had loved him as only a daughter can love a good man. Women have an instinct for that, even when they're young.

Yes, he'd been a religious man, but not a fanatic, not a wowser, and definitely not a self-righteous bigot. Rather the opposite. He had gone out of his way to help the under-privileged and those in trouble. His favourite quote from the Bible had been 'Pure religion and undefiled is this: to visit the fatherless and the widowed in their affliction.' And as he explained, that really meant anybody who was going through a rough time.

He was good at it, without preaching. Without seeking any glory for himself. And without looking for any reward.

So, as she grew up, Shirley began to help him. At first, she found it hard. Some of the people he helped seemed to be hopeless cases. But, as he explained, they were all God's children, however flawed, and all deserved a little respect and a helping hand.

As she matured, she became better at it, and became his trusted and efficient 'right hand'.

Then he died. What a shock! The whole town mourned. His funeral was the biggest seen in those parts in years. The tributes poured in. The hugs, the condolences, the tears, the genuine sympathy. But none of it brought him back.

His wife bore it stoically, but she had always been a background type and was content to fade from the public eye as soon as all the publicity died down.

It was then that Shirley knew she had to leave. Go to the big city. Get a job.

She got a job in an office complex and settled into a comfortable routine. But after a while, it was too comfortable. She felt unfulfilled, she needed more. So, falling back on her experiences with her father, she joined the Salvation Army and started going out with older members to help the down and outs on the streets; giving them soup, encouraging them to come to the designated shelter, generally giving them support and a little dignity.

She found she was good at it. Her father's influence and words of advice started paying dividends.

She became a regular at the shelter, spending all her spare time there. The vast majority of those needing help were men, many of them alcoholics, and – she had to admit to herself – some of them seemed beyond redemption. But that was not Salvation Army policy, nor had it been her father's. She quelled those thoughts and put equal energy into helping each person.

But one man did seem to stand out. At first glance, he didn't seem any different to the others, but Shirley felt that she could detect a subtle sensitivity in him; a sense of shame concerning what he had done and was doing, and an air about him that he could do better if only he could try just a little harder. She took to conversing with him, learnt that his wife had left him, taking their daughter with her, and that he had become addicted to drink in his despair.

He wasn't a professional man, just an ordinary worker, but she liked to sit and talk with him whenever she could. He wasn't crude like some of the other men; their conversations were interesting and she started to look forward to their times together.

Her influence, indirect and subtle, started to have its effect. He started shaving and washing more often, especially when he knew she would be coming. He cut out the clandestine drinking. He cut down on the smokes.

Their times together were always enjoyable and other people couldn't help but notice. The workers smiled tolerantly. It was not unusual for a man to have a shine on one of the younger female helpers, but the training the girls had received alerted them to the possible dangers and instructed them how to deal with it.

'Don't get emotionally involved,' they had been told. 'It's fine to be friendly, but realise what the other person is thinking.'

Shirley and the man sat and talked on every possible occasion. She asked him what religion he was and he said it wasn't anything particular. So she invited him to come along to a meeting. And of course he agreed. Anything to please her. He found it a bit boring but he was with her, wasn't he, so he was happy.

Then one day she told him that there was a job going at the office where she worked during the day. A cleaning job in the evening after most of the workers had gone home. Fine, he said, and so he started to earn a bit of money.

From his first pay packet, he bought her a gift as a token of gratitude. Not a feminine thing like a dress or a necklace, but a book. A good practical present that she could use.

He always found it fascinating that at church most people would sit in the same seat week after week. If you sat in someone else's place, there were scowls all round! He took to the same habit, sitting next to a young man on one side and, of course, Shirley on the other. The young man knew Shirley and often spoke to her across him. Not wishing to be offensive he sometimes invited the young man, whose name was Dennis, to share in their walks and talks. He made an intelligent addition to their discussions and it was obvious he liked the idea of chatting with Shirley.

One evening, after he had finished his cleaning shift, Shirley took him for a meal. They sat at the table in a quiet restaurant and, taking the bull by the horns, he asked her what she thought of Dennis.

'He's nice,' she said.

'Do you like him?'

'Yes, I like him.' A pause. 'But not like you.'

'How do you mean?'

'I love you.'

Silence, the tension hanging. Hanging.

'Oh, don't be silly,' he said at last. 'I'm too old.'

'That doesn't matter. I love you.'

'I think you're mistaking me for some sort of surrogate father.'

'Oh no. You're nothing like my father.'

He put his chin down to his chest, struggling for the right words. 'Shirley. Shirley, my very good friend. My saviour, if you like. Please don't do this. You know my background. I'm more than fifteen years older than you. You say you love me. Don't make me love you, because it would end in disaster.'

'Don't put yourself down, Laurie –'

'You know that my wife left me because of my drinking, don't you?'

'Of course I know. Did you ever get an official divorce?'

'No.'

'Then that's the first thing to do.'

'She took my daughter with her and I haven't seen them since. I don't want to put you through that.'

'You won't,' she said. 'You've stopped drinking. You're sensitive. You're intelligent. You do your job well, you're dependable.'

They left the restaurant and walked through the cold winter streets. She held his hand. The wind swirled through the gaps between the buildings and raised little eddies of dust.

'Laurie!' said Shirley. 'Come here.' They stepped into a doorway and she held him tight and wouldn't let him go. 'Laurie,' she said. 'It's time for you to move on. Start a new life. Get a new wife. Me.'

'Shirley, Shirley…' and then there were no more words said.

The soul has a language of its own. The spirit, which is a lesser version of the soul, will often shine through the eyes. But the soul speaks a deeper language and does not need words or sighs or looks. It is a form of meditation; it is a form of prayer; and perhaps it is the nearest we get to heaven whilst on this earth, this common ground, this vale of tears…..

Laurie and Shirley II

I'll buy you one more frozen orange juice on this fantastic day.
Peter Sarstedt

The other worshippers in the congregation used to smile indulgently at them. They would refer to them as 'you two', as though they were one entity. Holding hands: the older man whom they had seen could be decent if given a chance, and the young woman who had given him that very chance. Some of the old ladies wiped away a quiet tear, remembering their own time of being in love, of being aware of nothing else but each other, of not caring what anyone else thought.

The young man Dennis had been away for a few weeks and when he came back he found everything changed. Laurie and Shirley were an item, they were together, and Dennis felt out of it and had the good sense not to get in the way. Nonetheless, he felt lonely and missed their shared walks and conversations. While he had been away, he had thought of Shirley a lot and had determined to try to intensify their friendship. But now he saw that it was hopeless. She was besotted with Laurie and had no time for him. His heart was heavy and his shoulders drooped.

The weeks went by. Although it was only early spring and the wind was still cold, for two people it was already high summer.

Shirley recalled one day in particular when they went for a drive and ended up in a quiet rural village. They went into a little café near the park and ordered two soft drinks. The man behind the counter had a lined face and a big grey beard. He had owned and served behind the counter of his café for nearly thirty years, and he was tired of it. He sighed, weary of it all, as the couple sat at the table with the white cloth and drank their juice. He wished someone would come and buy his business. All he wanted out of life now was to sit in an easy chair and complain about the state of the world.

Laurie and Shirley left and walked through the park. The trees, still bare of leaves, had a stark beauty about them in the still air. They walked along the village street and admired the gardens. A cat sitting on a post purred and arched its back as they stroked it. They heard a toddler laughing as he played with his mother. They walked to the end of the village where the fields started, and a big old Clydesdale horse came trotting up to them, whinnying in friendship, the steam coming out of its nostrils. They pulled handfuls of grass and fed it; and a sheepdog came up to them, sat and held up its paw as if to shake hands.

They walked back through the village and Laurie plucked a flower, an early blooming yellow marigold, and handed it to her with a bow, grinning from ear to ear. She accepted with a mock curtsey and, laughing from the pits of their stomachs, they hugged each other in the middle of the street. Then he took it from her fingers and placed it in her chestnut coloured hair. They strolled on and a man, working in his garden, waved to them. A golden retriever sitting on a porch wagged its tail, its tongue just protruding from its open mouth. A blackbird sang in a tree. They walked along hand in hand, swinging their arms and giving the occasional skip, and giggling like fifteen-year-olds.

They went back into the café with the white tablecloths and ordered another drink. The words of a song came from the radio: I'll buy you one more frozen orange juice on this fantastic day… You rescue me, I rescue you.

'That's our song,' she said, and they leaned forward, grinning, and touched noses.

The old man with the lined face and big grey beard watched the couple as they sat at the table, the girl now looking radiant with a flower in her hair. He saw them say things quietly to each other and lean forward to touch noses, not kissing, just touching noses. And he smiled. It was the first time he had smiled in four years. When the couple had gone, the old man, still smiling to himself, walked into the back kitchen where his wife was working and he touched her hand.

The couple, Laurie and Shirley, stepped out of the café. The flower had gone a little askew in her hair and Laurie, in an act of extreme tenderness, put it straight again, gazing into her brown eyes. Then they held each other more quietly, more seriously, and for longer. They walked slowly back towards the car, holding each other tightly around the waist. Laurie, thirty-six years old and feeling twenty, and Shirley, twenty years old and feeling eighteen.

They sat on a nearby bench overlooking the park, still holding each other tight, her head on his shoulder. Laurie felt as though he had a halo around his head; and Shirley could hardly see straight for sheer love, love of this man, love of this moment, love of the whole world.

Wisps of smoke rose from a couple of chimneys in the late afternoon. A jogger came by and raised his hand in silent greeting. The blackbird sang on, a harbinger of warmth and life and contentment.

The light started to fade and it was time to go.

Shirley always thought of that village as a holy place, and of that day as a Gold and Purple Day.

Laurie and Shirley III

> Joy, whose hand is ever at his lips
> Bidding adieu.

Keats

It was six months now since he had started on the cleaning job. The boss had noticed his basic intelligence and had hinted of the chance to advance himself in the firm. Life was at last looking good. Six months! Time to celebrate!

He told her he wanted an early night but after she had left, he put on his coat and slipped round to the pub. It was a cold night and he felt the old pull of the comfortable warm bar room, filled with the smoke and the chatter of ordinary working men, men who liked a beer and were willing to share one with you. Especially if you were paying. He realised how much he'd missed it. The warmth, the friendly banter, the drink, the airy feeling of well-being, the raucous laughter, the dirty jokes, the back-slapping, and even if he felt his stomach wasn't quite up to it he drank on. He was celebrating, wasn't he, and these good men were helping him. My new friends. And when he told them he wasn't driving, then it was okay to have another couple of beers, wasn't it? Hoo-ey! What a night. What a bloody good night! Time for a piss, though, and when he came back, they had all gone. The bastards, I'll drink to their bad manners and another one just to see me home and the barman giving me a hard look well fuck him I'm celebrating something whatever it was and I'll be okay tomorrow even if I can't walk straight now goodnight you miserable bugger and I'm all right.

The cold air outside jerked his head back. He made it round the corner of the pub before the ground came up to hit him.

The barman, walking out to his car at the end of his shift, saw the prostrate figure on the ground and ignored him. He had seen so many drunks laid out that he didn't care any more. Fuck him, he reciprocated. Whatever he was celebrating must have been good.

Both policemen were young, but one, Henderson, had been on the force three years and was considered – at least by himself – to be experienced. Dumas, on the other hand, was a rookie. Less than two months on the job and still feeling inferior.

When they came upon the drunk on the road, Henderson immediately took charge. 'Just as well he rolled over,' he remarked, 'or he could have choked on his own vomit.'

Dumas shuddered.

'Come on,' said the other. 'Let's get him into the wagon. It's a night in the watch house for this idiot.'

The sun shone in a thin brittle way the next morning but Laurie felt as though it was the fires of hell. Upon release from the watch house and the departure of much of what was left of his money, he made his sad way home. He shuffled along, feeling terrible not only physically but spiritually. He knew that something – something – had come to an end. And he had an inkling what it was but he did not want to admit it to himself. Did not want to think about it.

He made it to his accommodation and sank onto his bed. 'I'm no good,' he thought. 'I'm just no bloody good.'

At work that evening, he seemed different. Somehow more relaxed, loose-limbed, but not in athletic or confident way.

The boss looked at him a few times before he realised what it was. The man's half drunk, he thought. How dare he! He called him into his office and, in the way of a good leader, said 'What's wrong, Laurie?'

'Whaddya mean?'

'Have you been drinking?'

'What's it to you?'

'Laurie –'

'I'm doing my job, aren't I? Don't bloody victimise me!'

'I'm not trying to victimise you, mate –'

'Mate?' he spat. 'Don't patronise me! I'm as good as you any day!'

'I'll get Shirley. Perhaps she can –'

'You leave Shirley out of it!' he yelled. 'You leave her out of it!'

But Shirley was at the door and came in with wide eyes.

'I told you to leave her out of it!' shouted the man. 'I don't want –'

'I didn't call her,' said the boss. 'She could see there was trouble.'

'Mr Roland,' said Shirley, 'let me speak to him. Please. Let me have a few minutes with him alone. I'll sort it out, I'm sure I can.'

'Well, if you think you can –'

But then Mr Roland's head was whipped back and he felt the sharp pain behind his left ear. He staggered and the anger came into his eyes. He pointed to the door. 'Out! Out!'

When the man was gone, Mr Roland tried to comfort the young lady. But he failed in that too. She wept and wept and he told her to go home and recover. After she left he sat down and felt behind his ear where the man had hit him. He fingered the pain, but it was only physical. There was a worse pain out there and he knew he could do nothing about it.

Julie

> Oh mother, tell your children
> Not to do what I have done.
>
> The Animals

I'm off men. They're all bastards. They're either weak or they're sleazebags. Fuck the lot of them. But not literally, I'm off that too. Should have been off years ago, tell the truth. But I'm definitely off now, since the abortion.

And the doctor was no better than the rest of them. When I told him I didn't know who the father was, he looked at me as if I was a common whore. And I'm not, I swear. I've accepted the occasional gift but I've never done it for money, honest.

It was all that bastard Dean's fault, when I think back. Fondling me and pawing me like that, and I was only fourteen.

And when I told my stepfather he just smiled and said, 'Well, you're an attractive girl.'

What a weakling! I don't know what mum saw in him, honest I don't. I'm sure my real father would have done something, if I'd known where he was.

And after Dean and his mate held me down, I had to get out of there. But life outside was no better. I just wanted someone to take care of me, to protect me, and all I got was bumpkins who were only after one thing.

Well, I needed food and shelter and it was the only thing I could give. I thought I might find someone who would look after me, perhaps even love me, but all I got was idiots. Zac, Greg, Tony or Terry, I forget what his name was, Darren, Alex, Drew, then that little Dutch guy, then Joe, then John – no, it was John then Joe, wasn't it? Not that it makes any difference. They were all deadbeats, lowlifes, and none of them had an ounce of affection in them. They all told me I was a good-looker, but that hasn't helped me; if I was plainer, perhaps they would have left me alone.

I'd thought that the Dutch guy – I wish I could remember his name – might love me a bit, because he gave me a dress and a necklace, but he turned out to be as ponderous and hopeless as the rest of them. And I would have preferred a book, truth be told.

Then when I went for the abortion and the doctor gave me that look, I knew I had to change. But I didn't know what to do. I did okay at school, I suppose, but when I ran away, I abandoned all that.

It was the worst time of all. Oh God! I just want someone to love me! Is that so hard?

Anyway, the abortion is over and I've been once to this counsellor who thinks she can help me. She's decent and she seems to understand. I get the feeling she's not too happy herself, but at least she's trying to do something constructive about it. Helping other people. Perhaps I can do that too. I've got nothing to lose, have I?

Shirley and Julie

> After all the loves of my life
> I'll be thinking of you,
> And wondering why?
>
> Richard Harris

So Shirley married Dennis. She insisted on a quiet wedding, just a few family and friends, and they said their vows on a rainy afternoon with about a dozen people attending.

And who's to say they were not happy?

Dennis was attentive, courteous, remembered her birthdays and their wedding anniversaries, and had a regular job, so they were not in need.

No children came along. As the years went by, the empty feeling in the pit of her stomach became a permanent feature.

She trained to become a counsellor, threw herself into her work and gained a good reputation. Helping other people meant that she did not have to face her own problems.

'But what problems could I have?' she asked herself. 'A good steady husband who is faithful, food on the table, and I'm in an honourable profession. So what's wrong?'

The problems her clients were having were much more severe. It made her grateful for what she had and gave her a sense of shame that she still felt unfulfilled.

Everyone has a lost love, she told herself, and she saw it all the time with her clients. It made her more sympathetic, more empathetic, and they sensed it and got some encouragement and hope from it.

Not all of them had a lost love, of course. Some had never been loved at all. Like the young girl who came to her after having had an abortion, who had been sexually abused when young and had run away, only to fall into bad company and continue a downward spiral. She wanted to get out of all that now, though, and Shirley took a special interest in her. There seemed to be a vague affiliation between the two of them, some instinctive feel that they were soulmates.

Shirley invited her along to the Salvation Army meetings and Julie went, holding Shirley's hand like a little child because she felt so insecure. She discovered she liked it. Here were people who shook your hand, even hugged you, who seemed interested in what you had to say and who didn't condemn you for past mistakes. She began looking forward to the meetings, feeling a sense of belonging, learning the names of the other members, and she started smiling – genuine smiles – for the first time in years. Life was at last looking better.

Shirley smiled at Julie's growing confidence but it only served to make her own situation feel worse. Her husband Dennis was growing more and more distant. He was still civil, never abusive, but after nine years, where was the passion, the sense of fun, the little looks and touches that loving people should have?

After nine years of marriage, of course, they had few secrets from each other. But in a special place that Dennis did not know about, Shirley had a little wooden box and inside it was a perfectly dried and preserved yellow marigold.

One winter's afternoon with a dry cold wind, Dennis came home from work and seemed more nervous than usual. Shirley had long grown insensitive to his moods and dully prepared the evening meal.

They ate in silence. It was not unusual.

When they had finished, Dennis took a deep breath and said, 'Shirley, I want a divorce.'

She looked up sharply. 'Why?'

Her upbringing and her allegiance to the church still made divorce anathema to her thinking. Even if something inside her told her this was the way forward.

'It's not working, is it? he said.

At least the man was honest.

She bowed her head and the tears fell. But it was not tears for herself. It was tears for the institute of marriage, which she had held so dear, and she knew she would agree with the man sitting opposite her. 'You're a good man,' she said. 'Honest. Hard-working. Faithful. But you're right. You're right.'

'Neither of us is in the wrong,' he said, 'but neither of us is happy. Let's not worry about what other people think.'

'Have you got another woman?'

'No. But I want the chance to meet someone.'

She lay in bed that night and thought about her life. It had not been miserable by any means, but there had been few moments of deep ecstasy, of high passion, that everyone – she thought – is supposed to have.

She thought of the one man she had truly loved. She thought of her secret box and the flower inside it, and of that Gold and Purple Day he had placed it in her hair, and the hot tears soaked her pillow.

Well, a divorce. With no shame attached. A divorce. Freedom!

What now? Think forward, she told herself, and that was more difficult than she imagined. It was so easy to dwell on the past. But that was useless. It was the sort of thing she was always telling her clients. Accept the past with all its broken dreams and move forward. Now she needed that counselling for herself.

She would just throw herself more into her work and be of some use to humanity in that way. The girl Julie, for example, was a real convert. It was time to ask her to come out with her in the evenings, when they went to visit the down-and-outs to try and help them.

Prognosis

You rescue me, I rescue you.

Peter Sarstedt

They arranged for the following Friday. Shirley gave her a couple of lessons over the previous days; what to say and what to do, and what not to say and do.

Nevertheless, Shirley felt apprehensive. Julie was still a young girl, barely twenty. Certainly not innocent but definitely not experienced in what they were undertaking. But everyone's got to start somewhere, she told herself. I was lucky with my father bringing me up like that.

She greeted Julie with a smile and they climbed into the car ready for their rounds.

'We'll go by the big grocery warehouse first,' she said. 'There's often some men there who need help.'

As they drove, the radio played in the car. A song came on: I'll buy you one more frozen orange juice on this fantastic day… I pick a flower from the road and place it in your heart… You rescue me, I rescue you.

Shirley leaned over quickly and snapped off the radio. Julie looked up in surprise at her companion and noticed her chin was trembling.

After a little while, Shirley took a deep quivering breath and said, 'Did I ever tell you I had a lost love? An older man. But I didn't marry him.'

'Why not?'

Again it was a while before Shirley found the words.

'It didn't work out.'

And Julie, to her immense credit, kept quiet.

They arrived at the big grocery warehouse and pulled up.

They said a quick prayer, then 'Okay,' said the older woman. 'Come on, let's see what we can do for those three over there under the fire escape.'

But as they approached, two of the men looked up and quickly slipped away around the corner, leaving their companion slumped against the wall.

'He looks a hopeless case,' said Julie.

'Nobody's a hopeless case,' said Shirley.

So the two women approached the man, whose chin had fallen on his chest, his tongue lolling out, a dribble of saliva running onto his coat and his cheeks slightly moist.

Motor neurone disease (MND) is the name given to a group of diseases in which the nerve cells (neurones) controlling the muscles that enable us to move, speak, breathe and swallow undergo degeneration and die. With no nerves to activate them, muscles gradually weaken and waste. MND can affect a person's ability to walk, speak, swallow and breathe. Each day in Australia, two people die from MND. There is no known cure and no effective treatment for MND.

The Motor Neurone Disease Association of Tasmania assists people living with MND by providing information, equipment, raising the profile of MND in the community and raising funds for research into MND.